FRIEDRICH DÜRRENMATT

THE

PUSHKIN VERTIGO

PLEDGE

REQUIEM FOR THE DETECTIVE NOVEL

Pushkin Vertigo
71–75 Shelton Street
London, WC2H 9JQ

Original text © 1986 by Diogenes Verlag AG, Zurich
English translation by Joel Agee © 2000
by Diogenes Verlag AG, Zurich

The Pledge was first published by Verlag der
Arche as *Das Versprechen* in Zurich, 1958

First published in English by Jonathan Cape, 1959

First published by Pushkin Press in 2017

3 5 7 9 8 6 4

ISBN 978 1 782273 39 4

Text designed and typeset by Tetragon, London
Printed and bound by CPI Group (UK) Ltd, Croydon CRO 4YY

www.pushkinpress.com

Whose dark or troubled mind will you step into next? Detective or assassin, victim or accomplice? How can you tell reality from delusion when you're spinning in the whirl of a thriller, or trapped in the grip of an unsolvable mystery? When you can't trust your senses, or anyone you meet; that's when you know you're in the hands of the undisputed masters of crime fiction.

Writers of the greatest thrillers and mysteries on earth, who inspired those that followed. Their books are found on shelves all across their home countries – from Asia to Europe, and everywhere in between. Timeless tales that have been devoured, adored and handed down through the decades. Iconic books that have inspired films, and demand to be read and read again. And now we've introduced Pushkin Vertigo Originals – the greatest contemporary crime writing from across the globe, by some of today's best authors.

So step inside a dizzying world of criminal masterminds with **Pushkin Vertigo**. The only trouble you might have is leaving them behind.

1

Last March I had to give a lecture in Chur on the art of writing detective stories. My train pulled in just before nightfall, under low clouds, in a dreary blizzard. As if that wasn't enough, the roads were paved with ice. The lecture was being held in the hall of the Chamber of Commerce. There wasn't much of an audience, since Emil Staiger was lecturing in the school auditorium about Goethe's late period. I couldn't summon up the right mood, and neither could anyone else; several local residents left the room before I had ended my talk. After a brief chat with some members of the board of directors, two or three high-school teachers who also would have preferred the late Goethe, and a philanthropic lady who volunteered her services as manager of the Domestic Workers Alliance of Eastern Switzerland, I received my fee and traveling expenses and withdrew to the room I had been given at the Hotel Steinbock, near the train station—another dismal place. Except for a German financial newspaper and an old illustrated magazine, I couldn't find anything to read. The silence of the hotel was inhuman. Impossible to even think of falling asleep, because that would give rise to the fear of not waking again. A timeless, spectral night. It had stopped snowing outside, no movement anywhere, the street lamps were no longer swaying, not a puff of wind, no denizen of Chur, no animal,

7

nothing at all, except for a single heaven-rending blast from the train station. I went to the bar to have another whiskey. There, in addition to the elderly barmaid, I found a man who introduced himself the moment I sat down. He was Dr. H., the former chief of police in the canton of Zurich, a large and heavy man, old-fashioned, with a gold watch chain running across his vest. Despite his age, his bristly hair was still black, his mustache bushy. He was sitting on one of the high chairs by the bar, drinking red wine, smoking a Bahianos, and addressing the barmaid by her first name. His voice was loud and his gestures were lively, a blunt and unfastidious sort of person who simultaneously attracted and repelled me. When it was nearly three o'clock and our first Johnnie Walker had been followed by four more, he offered to drive me to Zurich the next morning in his Opel Kapitän. Since I did not know the area around Chur or that whole part of Switzerland, I accepted the invitation. Dr. H. had come to Graubünden as a member of a federal commission, and since the weather had prevented his departure, he, too, had attended my lecture, about which he had nothing to say beyond remarking that I had "a rather awkward delivery."

We set out the next morning. At dawn, I had taken two Medomins to catch a little sleep, and now I felt virtually paralyzed. The day seemed still dark, though the sun had risen a while ago. There was a patch of metallic sky gleaming somewhere through a covering of dense, sluggishly lumbering, snow-filled clouds. Winter seemed unwilling to leave this part of the country. The city was surrounded by mountains, but there was nothing majestic about them; they rather resembled heaps of earth, as though someone had dug an immense grave. Chur itself was quite evidently made of stone, gray, with large government buildings. It seemed incredible to me that this was a wine-growing region. We tried to penetrate into the old inner city, but the heavy car strayed into a network of narrow lanes and one-way streets, and only a complex maneuver in reverse gear got us out of the tangle of houses. Moreover, the streets were icy, so we were glad to have the city behind us at last, although I had seen almost nothing of this old episcopal residence. It was like a flight. I dozed, feeling leaden and weary; vaguely, through the low scuttling clouds, I saw a snow-covered valley gliding past us, rigid with cold. I don't know for how long. Then we were driving toward a large village, perhaps a small town, carefully, and suddenly everything was illuminated by sunlight so powerful and blinding that the snowy planes began to melt. A white ground mist rose, spreading imperceptibly over the snowfields until, once again, the valley was hidden from my sight. It was like a bad dream, like an evil spell, as if I was not supposed to experience these mountains. My weariness came back. The gravel with which the road had been strewn clattered unpleasantly; driving over a bridge, we went into a slight skid; then we passed a military transport; the windshield became so dirty that the wipers could no longer clean it. H. sat sullenly next to me at the wheel, absorbed in his own thoughts, concentrating on the difficult road. I regretted having accepted his invitation, cursed the whiskey and my sleeping pills. But gradually, things improved. The valley became visible again, and more human, too. There were farms everywhere, and occasionally a small factory, everything spare and clean, the road free of snow and ice now, glistening with wetness, but safe enough for us to accelerate to a decent speed. The mountains no longer hemmed us in from all sides but had opened out, and then we stopped next to a gas station.

The house immediately struck me as peculiar, perhaps because it stood out from its neat and proper surroundings. It was a wretched-looking thing with streams of water flowing down its sides. Half of it was made of stone; the other half was a wooden shed whose front wall was covered with posters. Evidently this had been its use for a long time, for there were whole layers of posters pasted one over the other: *Burrus Tobacco for Modern Pipes, Drink Canada Dry, Sport Mints, Vitamins, Lindt's Milk Chocolate,* and so on. On the side wall, in giant letters: *Pirelli Tires.* The two gas pumps stood on an uneven, badly paved square in front of the house; everything made a run-down impression, despite the sun, which was now exuding a stinging heat that seemed almost malevolent.

"Let's get out," said the former chief of police, and I obeyed without understanding what he had in mind, but glad to step into the fresh air.

Next to the open door sat an old man on a stone bench. He was unshaven and unwashed, wore a pale smock that was smeared and stained, and dark, grease-spotted trousers that had once been part of a tuxedo. Old slippers on his feet. His eyes were staring, stupefied, and I could smell the liquor from afar. Absinthe. The pavement around the stone bench was littered with cigarette butts that were floating in puddles of melted snow.

"Hello," said the police chief, and he suddenly sounded embarrassed. "Full up, please. Super. And clean the windshields." Then he turned to me. "Let's go in."

Only now did I notice a tavern sign over the only visible window, a red metal disk. And over the door was the name of the place: *Zur Rose*. We stepped into a dirty corridor. The stench of beer and schnapps. The chief walked ahead of me. He opened a wooden door; evidently he had been here before. The barroom was dark and dingy, a couple of rough-hewn tables and benches, the walls papered with cutout pictures of movie stars; the Austrian radio was giving a market report for the Tyrol, and behind the counter, barely discernible, stood a haggard woman in a dressing gown, smoking a cigarette and washing glasses.

"Two coffees with cream," said the chief.

The woman went about preparing the coffee. From the adjoining room came a sloppy-looking waitress who looked about thirty years old to me.

"She's sixteen," the chief muttered.

The girl served us our coffees. She was wearing a black skirt and a white, half-open blouse, with nothing underneath; her skin was unwashed. She was blond, as the woman behind the counter must once have been, and her hair was uncombed.

"Thank you, Annemarie," the chief said, and laid the money on the table. The girl, too, did not reply, did not even thank him. We drank in silence. The coffee was awful. The chief lit himself a Bahianos. The Austrian radio was now discussing the water level and the girl shuffled off to the room next door, where we saw something whitish shimmering, probably an unmade bed.

11

"Let's go," said the chief.

Outside, after a glance at the pump, he paid the old man for filling the tank and cleaning the windshields.

"Next time," the chief said by way of farewell, and again I noticed his helpless air; but the old man still didn't reply; he was back on his bench, staring into space, stupefied, obliterated. When we had reached the Opel and turned around again, the old man was clenching his fists, shaking them, and whispering, pressing the words out in brief, forceful gasps, his face transfigured by an immense faith: "I'll wait, I'll wait, he'll come, he'll come."

2

"To be honest," Dr. H. began later as we were approaching the Kerenz Pass—the road was icy again, and beneath us lay Lake Walen, glittering, cold, forbidding; also, the leaden weariness from the Medomin had come back, the memory of the smoky taste of the whiskey, the feeling of gliding along in an endless, meaningless dream—"to be honest, I have never thought highly of detective novels and I rather regret that you, too, write them. It's a waste of time. Though what you said in your lecture yesterday was worth hearing; since the politicians have shown themselves to be so criminally inept—and it takes one to know one, I'm a member of Parliament, as I'm sure you're aware...." (I had no idea, I was listening to his voice as if from a great distance, barricaded behind my tiredness, but attentive, like an animal in its lair.)

"...People hope the police at least will know how to put the world in order, which strikes me as the most miserable thing you could possibly hope for. But unfortunately, these mystery stories perpetrate a whole different sort of deception. I don't even mean the fact that your criminals are always brought to justice. It's a nice fairy tale and is probably morally necessary. It's one of those lies that preserve the state, like that pious homily 'crime doesn't pay'—when all that's required to test this particular piece of wisdom is to have a good look at human

13

society; no, I'd let all that pass, for business reasons if nothing else, because every reader and every taxpayer has a right to his heroes and his happy end, and it's our job to deliver that—I mean ours as policemen, just as much as it's your job as writers. No, what really bothers me about your novels is the story line, the plot. There the lying just takes over, it's shameless. You set up your stories logically, like a chess game: here's the criminal, there's the victim, here's an accomplice, there's a beneficiary; and all the detective needs to know is the rules, he replays the moves of the game, and checkmate, the criminal is caught and justice has triumphed. This fantasy drives me crazy. You can't come to grips with reality by logic alone. Granted, we of the police are forced to proceed logically, scientifically; but there is so much interference, so many factors mess up our clear schemes, that success in our business very often amounts to no more than professional luck and pure chance working in our favor. Or against us. But in your novels, chance plays no part, and if something looks like chance, it's made out to be some kind of fate or providence; the truth gets thrown to the wolves, which in your case are the dramatic rules. Get rid of them, for God's sake. Real events can't be resolved like a mathematical formula, for the simple reason that we never know all the necessary factors, just a few, and usually a rather insignificant few. And chance—the incalculable, the incommensurable—plays too great a part. Our laws are based only on probability, on statistics, not on causality; they apply to the general rule, not the particular case. The individual can't be grasped by calculation. Our criminological methods are inadequate, and the more we

14

refine them, the more inadequate they get. But you fellows in the writing game don't care about that. You don't try to grapple with a reality that keeps eluding us, you just set up a manageable world. That world may be perfect, but it's a lie. Forget about perfection if you want to make headway and get at the way things actually are, at reality, like a man; otherwise you'll be left fiddling around with useless stylistic exercises. But let's get to the point.

"I'm sure you were surprised by a few things this morning. First of all, by my own talk; a former chief of the Zurich cantonal police should express more moderate views. But I am old and I've stopped lying to myself. I know very well what a dubious bunch we all are, how little we can accomplish, how easily we make mistakes; but I also know that we have to act anyway, even at the risk of acting wrongly.

"Then you must also have wondered why I stopped at that miserable gas station, and I'll confess it to you right away: that pathetic drunken wreck who filled up our tank used to be my most capable man. God knows I knew something about my profession, but Matthäi was a genius, and this to a degree that puts all your paper detectives to shame.

"The story happened almost nine years ago," H. continued after passing a Shell oil truck. "Matthäi was one of my inspectors, or rather, one of my first lieutenants—we use military ranks in the cantonal police. He was a lawyer, like me, a Baseler who had taken his doctorate in Basel, and among certain groups that made his acquaintance 'professionally,' his nickname was 'Dead-end Matthäi.' After a while we called him that, too. He was a lonely man, always neatly dressed,

15

impersonal, formal, aloof; he didn't smoke, didn't drink, but on the job he was tough as nails, downright ruthless, and as hated as he was successful. I was never able to figure him out. I think I was the only person he liked—because I have a soft spot for clearheaded people, even though his lack of humor often got on my nerves. He was extremely bright, but the all too solid structures in our country had made him emotionless. He was what you'd call an organization man, and he used the police apparatus like a slide rule. He wasn't married, he never spoke of his private life—probably he didn't have one. The only thing he thought about was his job. He was a top-notch detective, but he worked without passion. He was stubborn, tireless, but when you watched him in action, he appeared to be bored; until one day he got embroiled in a case that suddenly stirred him to passion.

"He was at the pinnacle of his career at the time. There had been some difficulties with him in the department. I was going to be retired, and my most likely successor was Matthäi. But there were obstacles to his appointment that couldn't be ignored. Not only that he didn't belong to any party, but the rank and file would have objected. The cantonal government, on the other hand, was hesitant to pass over such a capable man. So when the government of Jordan asked the federal government to send an expert to Amman to reorganize their police, it was like a godsend: Matthäi was recommended by Zurich and accepted by Berne and Amman. Everyone heaved a sigh of relief. He, too, was pleased, and not just for professional reasons. He was about fifty then—a little desert sun would do him good, he figured; he looked forward to the trip, to the flight across the Alps and the Mediterranean; probably he imagined this would be his final farewell from us, for he hinted that afterward he would move to Denmark to live with a widowed sister there—and he was just clearing out his desk in the cantonal police headquarters on Kasernenstrasse when the call came."

3

"Matthäi had a hard time making sense of that jumbled report," the chief continued. "It was one of his old 'clients' calling from Mägendorf, a little hole in the wall near Zurich. The man was a peddler named von Gunten. Matthäi wasn't really in the mood to take up this case on his last afternoon on the job. He had already bought his plane ticket, he'd be leaving in three days. But I was away at a conference of police chiefs and wasn't expected back from Berne until evening. This case called for competent handling; inexperience could spoil everything. Matthäi called the police station in Mägendorf. It was near the end of April, buckets of rain splashing down outside, the föhn had blown into the city, but the nasty, malignant heat persisted, and people could hardly breathe.

"Officer Riesen picked up the phone.

"'Is it raining in Mägendorf, too?' Matthäi asked, ill-humored, even though he could guess the answer, and when he heard it, his face looked even gloomier. Then he gave the man instructions to keep an inconspicuous watch on the peddler who was staying at The Stag in Mägendorf.

"Matthäi hung up.

"'Something happen?' Feller asked curiously. He was helping his boss pack his belongings—mainly books, which Matthäi had accumulated over the years, a whole library.

"'It's raining in Mägendorf, too,' the inspector replied. 'Get the emergency squad ready.'

"'Murder?'

"'Damned rain,' Matthäi muttered in place of an answer, indifferent to Feller's hurt feelings.

"But before he joined the examining magistrate and Lieutenant Henzi, who were waiting impatiently in their car, he leafed through von Gunten's dossier. The man had a record. Sexual molestation of a fourteen-year-old girl."

4

"That very first order to have the peddler watched turned out to be a mistake that could not have been foreseen. Mägendorf was a small community. Mostly farmers, though some men worked in the factories down in the valley or in the brick-yard nearby. There were a few city people living out there, two or three architects, a neoclassical sculptor, but they played no part in the village. Everyone knew everyone else, and most people were related. The village was in conflict with the city, not officially, but secretly; for the woods surrounding Mägendorf belonged to the city, a fact which no real Mägendorfer had ever taken into account, to the great annoyance of the forest administration, who finally insisted that a police station be set up in Mägendorf. And there was another problem: on Sundays, people came streaming in from the city and took over the village; and many others were drawn to The Stag at night. With all these factors to consider, the man stationed there had to be a capable police-man, but he also had to be on good terms with the village. Officer Wegmüller, who was assigned there, understood this fairly quickly. He came from a peasant family, drank a lot, and kept his Mägendorfers well in hand, though he made so many concessions that I really should have intervened; but to me—in part because of our shortage of manpower—he was the lesser evil. I had my peace and I let Wegmüller have his. It was his substitutes—when he was on leave—who were put through the mill. As far as the Mägendorfers were concerned, they couldn't do anything right. Those were boom times, no one went poaching or stealing wood in the forests, and there hadn't been a brawl in the village for ages, but you could still feel the traditional defiance of state power smoldering among the people. Riesen, in particular, had a rough time. He was a simpleminded fellow, humorless, easily offended, no match for the villagers' constant mocking, and really too sensitive even for a more normal area. He was so intimidated that he would make himself scarce as soon as he was done with his daily rounds. Under such conditions it proved impossible to keep an 'inconspicuous watch' on the peddler. Riesen usually stayed far away from The Stag, so his sudden appearance there had all the weight of a federal inquest. And when he ostentatiously took a seat facing the peddler, the farmers fell into a silence that was humming with curiosity.

"'Coffee?' the innkeeper asked.

"'Nothing,' Riesen replied. 'I'm here on duty.'

"The farmers stared at the peddler.

"'What did he do?' an old man asked.

"'None of your business.'

"The tavern was low and filled with smoke, a wooden cave, oppressively hot and dark, but the innkeeper didn't turn on the light. The farmers sat at a long table, perhaps over white wine, perhaps over beer, invisible except as shadows against the silvery windowpanes with their trickles and streams of rainwater. From somewhere came the clatter of a game of

21

table soccer; from somewhere else, the ringing and rumbling sounds of an American pinball machine.

"Von Gunten was drinking a cherry liqueur. He was afraid. He sat hunched in a corner, his right arm propped on the handle of his basket, waiting. It seemed to him that he had been sitting there for hours. Everything was densely quiet, but menacing. The windowpanes started lightening, the rain lessened, and suddenly the sun was out again. Only the wind was still howling and shaking the walls. Von Gunten was glad when the cars finally pulled up outside.

"'Come,' said Riesen, getting up. The two men stepped outside. In front of the tavern stood a dark limousine and the emergency squad's big van. The ambulance was on its way. The village square lay in the glaring sun. Two five- or six-year- old children stood by the well, a girl and a boy. The girl had a doll tucked under one arm, and the boy was holding a little whip.

"'Get in next to the driver, von Gunten!' Matthäi called from the window of the limousine, and then, when the peddler had taken his seat with a sigh of relief (as if he were safe now), and Riesen had climbed into the other car: 'All right, now show us what you found in the woods.'"

5

"After a short walk through wet grass—the path to the woods was a single muddy puddle—they found the small body in the leaves among the bushes not far from the edge of the forest. The men were silent. The storm was still lashing the treetops and shaking loose large silver drops that glittered like diamonds. The public prosecutor tossed away his cigar and stepped on it, embarrassed. Henzi didn't dare to look. Matthäi said: 'A police officer never looks away, Henzi.'

"The men set up their cameras.

"'It'll be hard to find tracks after this rain,' Matthäi said. "Suddenly the boy and the girl were standing in their midst, staring at the body, the girl still with her doll under her arm, the boy still with his whip.

"'Take the children away.'

"A policeman took them by the hand and led them back to the road, and there they stayed.

"The first people from the village approached. The owner of The Stag was recognizable from afar by his white apron.

"'Cordon her off,' the inspector ordered. Several men posted themselves as guards. Others searched the immediate vicinity. Then the first flashbulbs went off.

"'Do you know the girl, Riesen?'

"'No, sir, I don't.'

"'Did you ever see her in the village?'

"'I believe I have, sir.'

"'Has the girl been photographed?'

"'Two more shots from above.'

"Matthäi waited.

"'Tracks?'

"'Nothing. Everything's mud.'

"'Check the buttons? Fingerprints?'

"'Hopeless after this cloudburst.'

"Then Matthäi carefully bent over. 'With a razor,' he noted, picked up the pieces of bread strewn about and carefully put them back in the little basket.

"'Pretzels.'

"News came that someone from the village wanted to talk to them. Matthäi stood up. The investigating magistrate looked over toward the edge of the woods. There stood a white-haired man with an umbrella hanging from his left forearm. Henzi was leaning against a beech tree. He was pale. The peddler sat on his basket, quietly repeating, over and over, with a soft voice: 'I just happened to pass by here, just by chance!'

"'Bring the man here.'

"The white-haired man came through the bushes and froze.

"'My God,' he murmured, 'my God.'

"'May I ask for your name?' Matthäi asked.

"'I am the teacher Luginbühl,' the white-haired man replied, and looked away.

"'Do you know this girl?'

"'It's Gritli Moser.'

"'Where do her parents live?'

"'Down in the Moosbach.'

"'Far from the village?'

"'Fifteen minutes.'

"Matthäi looked at the body. He was the only one who didn't flinch. No one said a word.

"'How did this happen?' the teacher asked.

"'A sex crime,' Matthäi replied. 'Did the child go to your school?'

"'To Fräulein Krumm's class. Third grade.'

"'Do the Mosers have any other children?'

"'Gritli was the only one.'

"'Someone has to tell the parents.'

"The men fell silent again.

"'You, sir?" Matthäi asked the teacher.

"There was a long pause before Luginbühl replied. 'Please don't consider me a coward,' he finally said, hesitantly, 'but I would rather not. I can't,' he quietly added.

"'I understand,' Matthäi said. 'How about the pastor?'

"'He's in the city.'

"'All right,' Matthäi calmly said. 'You may leave, Herr Luginbühl.'

"The teacher went back to the road. More and more people from Mägendorf had assembled there.

"Matthäi looked over at Henzi, who was still leaning against the beech tree. 'Please, no, sir,' Henzi said softly. The investigating magistrate also shook his head. Matthäi looked at the body once more, and then glanced at the little red skirt lying torn in the bushes, soaked through with blood and rain.

"'Then I'll go,' he said, and picked up the basket of pretzels."

6

"The 'Moosbach' was a small marshy dale near Mägendorf. Matthäi had left the police car in the village and walked. He wanted to gain time. He could see the house from far away. He stopped and turned around. He had heard footsteps. The little boy and the girl were there again, with flushed faces. They must have taken shortcuts; there was no other way to explain their reappearance.

"Matthäi walked on. The house was low, with white walls, dark beams, and a slate roof. Fig trees behind it, black soil in the garden. A man was chopping wood in front of the house. He looked up and saw the inspector approaching.

"'What can I do for you?' the man said.

"Matthäi hesitated, unsure how to proceed. Then he introduced himself, just to gain time. 'Herr Moser?'

"'That's me, what do you want?' the man said again. He came closer and stood in front of Matthäi with his ax in his hand. He must have been about forty. He was lean, with a furrowed face, and his gray eyes scrutinized the inspector. A woman appeared in the doorway; she, too, was wearing a red skirt. Matthäi searched for words. All along on his walk he had been searching for the right formulation, but he still didn't know what to say. Then Moser came to his aid. He had noticed the basket in Matthäi's hand.

"'Did something happen to Gritli?' he asked, his eyes probing Matthäi's face again.

"'Did you send Gritli somewhere?' the inspector asked.

"'To her grandmother in Fehren,' the farmer replied.

"Matthäi reflected; Fehren was the neighboring village. 'Did Gritli go that way often?' he asked.

"'Every Wednesday and Saturday afternoon,' the farmer said. Then, in a sudden rush of fear, he asked: 'Why do you want to know? Why are you bringing her basket?'

"Matthäi put the basket on the stump on which Moser had been chopping wood.

"'Gritli has been found dead in the woods near Mägendorf,' he said.

"Moser did not move. Nor did the woman, who was still standing in the doorway in her red skirt. Matthäi saw beads of perspiration form on the man's forehead; a moment later sweat was streaming down his white face. Matthäi would have liked to look away, but he was spellbound by this face, by this sweat, and so they stood staring at each other.

"'Gritli was murdered,' Matthäi heard himself say, with a voice that seemed devoid of compassion. This annoyed him.

"'It can't be,' Moser whispered, 'there can't be such devils.' The fist holding the ax was quivering.

"'There are such devils, Herr Moser,' Matthäi said.

"The man stared at him.

"'I want to see my child,' he said almost inaudibly.

"The inspector shook his head. 'I wouldn't do that, Herr Moser. I know it's a cruel thing to say, but it's better if you don't go to your Gritli now.'

27

"Moser stepped up very close to the inspector, so close that the two men stood eye to eye.

"'Why is it better?' he shouted.

"The inspector said nothing.

"For a moment Moser weighed the ax in his hand as though he wanted to strike out with it, but then he turned away and went to his wife, who was still standing in the doorway. Still motionless, still mute. Matthäi waited. Nothing escaped him, and he suddenly knew he would never forget this scene. Moser clasped his wife in his arms. He was suddenly shaken by a silent sob. He hid his face against her shoulder while she stared into space.

"'Tomorrow evening you may see your Gritli,' the inspector promised. He felt feeble, helpless. 'By then the child will look as if she's asleep.'

"Then the woman suddenly spoke.

"'Who is the murderer?' she asked in a voice so calm and sober that Matthäi was startled.

"'I intend to find that out, Frau Moser.'

"The woman just looked at him. Her gaze was threatening, imperious. 'Is that a promise?'

"'It's a promise, Frau Moser,' the inspector said, impelled solely by the desire to leave this place.

"'On your eternal salvation?'

"The inspector hesitated. 'On my eternal salvation,' he finally said. What else could he do?

"'Then go,' the woman commanded. 'You have sworn by your eternal salvation.'

"Matthäi wanted to add a consoling word, but he could think of no consolation.

"'I'm sorry,' he said softly, and turned around. Slowly he walked back the way he had come. Before him lay Mägendorf with the forest behind it. Above, the sky, which was cloudless now. He saw the two children again, crouching by the side of the road. He walked past them wearily, and they followed with quick, tripping steps. Then suddenly he heard from the house behind him a sound like the bellow of an animal. He hurried his steps, and did not know whether it was the man or the woman who was crying so."

"Back in Mägendorf, Matthäi met with his first difficulty. The emergency squad's large van had driven into the village and was waiting for the inspector. The scene of the crime and its immediate vicinity had been carefully searched and then cordoned off. Three plainclothes policemen were hiding in the woods. Their assignment was to observe passersby. The rest of the squad was to be taken back to the city. The sky was swept clean, but the rain hadn't eased up the atmosphere. The föhn still lay heavily upon the forests and villages, still came wafting along in great soft gusts. The unnatural heavy warmth made people spiteful, irritable, impatient. The street lamps were already lit, even though it was still day. The farmers had been massing together. They had discovered von Gunten. They considered him to be the murderer; peddlers are always suspect. They assumed he had already been arrested and surrounded the van. The peddler inside kept quiet. Trembling, he cowered among the stiffly upright policemen. The Mägendorfers moved more and more closely against the van, pressing their faces against the windows. The policemen didn't know what to do. The state prosecutor's limousine was also being blocked by the crowd. So was the coroner's car, which had come in from Zurich. So was the white ambulance containing the little corpse. The men looked threatening but were silent; the women stood pressed against the walls of the houses. They, too, were silent. The children had climbed onto the rim of the village fountain. A dark rage without plan or direction had bonded the farmers into a mob. They wanted revenge, justice. Matthäi tried to fight his way through to the emergency squad, but this was not possible. The best thing would be to find the mayor. He asked for him. No one answered. All he could hear were a few quiet threats. The inspector reflected and went into the tavern. He wasn't mistaken, the mayor was sitting in The Stag. He was a small, heavy man with an unhealthy appearance. He was drinking one glass of Veltliner after another and peering through the low windows.

"'What can I do, Inspector?' he asked. 'The people are stubborn. They feel that the police aren't thorough enough, and that they have to take care of justice.' Then he sighed: 'Gritli was a good child. We loved her.'

"The mayor had tears in his eyes.

"'The peddler is innocent,' Matthäi said.

"'If he was, you wouldn't have arrested him.'

"'We haven't arrested him. We need him as a witness.'

"The major fixed a baleful look on Matthäi. 'You're just trying to talk your way out of it,' he said. 'We know what's going on.'

"'As mayor, your first obligation is to ensure our free passage.'

"The mayor emptied his glass of red wine. He drank without saying a word.

"'Well?' Matthäi asked impatiently.

31

"The mayor remained stubborn.

"'The peddler's going to get it,' he mumbled.

"The inspector made himself clear. 'There would be a fight before that happened, sir—Mr. Mayor of Mägendorf.'

"'You want to fight for a sex fiend?'

"'Guilty or not, we'll have law and order here.'

"The mayor angrily walked back and forth in the low-ceilinged tavern room. Since no one was there to serve him, he poured wine for himself at the bar. He drank it so hastily that large dark stripes ran over his shirt. The crowd was still quiet outside. But when the driver tried to set the police car in motion, the ranks closed more tightly.

"Now the public prosecutor entered the room. He had squeezed through the tightly packed crowd with difficulty. His clothes were rumpled. The mayor was alarmed. The arrival of a public prosecutor put him on edge; being a normal person, he found this profession uncanny.

"'Mr. Mayor,' the public prosecutor said, 'the Mägendorfers seem to want to resort to a lynching. I don't see any other way out than to call for reinforcements. That should bring them back to reason.'

"'Let's try to talk to them once more,' Matthäi suggested.

"The public prosecutor tapped the mayor with his right index finger.

"'If you don't get these people to listen to us, and I mean right away, you'll be sorry.'

"Outside, the church bells started ringing up a storm. More and more men came from all directions to join the crowd. Even the fire squad marched in and took up fighting positions in support of their townsmen. The first shrill, isolated shouts rang out, curses directed at the police.

"The policemen readied themselves. They expected the crowd to attack any minute, but they were as helpless as the Mägendorfers. Their usual activities were a combination of routine patrols and individual assignments; here they were confronting something unknown. But the agitated farmers became suddenly quieter. The public prosecutor had stepped out of The Stag with the mayor and Matthäi. Using a stair in front of the tavern door as a platform, holding on to an iron banister, the mayor addressed the mob: 'Citizens of Mägendorf! I ask you to listen to His Honor, Public Prosecutor Burkhard.'

"There was no visible reaction in the crowd. The farmers and workers stood again as before, silent, threatening, motionless under the sky, which was putting on the first shining lights of the evening; street lamps swayed over the square like pale moons. The Mägendorfers were determined to seize the man they took to be the murderer. The police cars stood like large dark beasts, at bay in this human tide. Again and again they attempted to break loose, the motors roared and howled, then subsided, discouraged, and were turned off again. No use. The whole village—the dark gables, the square, the crowd in its uncertainty and rage—staggered under the burden of the day's event, as if the murder had poisoned the world.

"'People,' the public prosecutor began, in a low, uncertain voice, but every word was audible, 'Mägendorfers, we are shocked by this horrible crime. Gritli Moser has been murdered. We don't know who committed the crime. . . .'

"The public prosecutor got no further than that.

33

"'Hand him over!'

"Fists were raised, whistles rang out.

"Matthäi watched the mob, spellbound.

"'Quick, Matthäi!' the public prosecutor barked. 'Call for reinforcements!'

"'Von Gunten is the killer!' screamed a tall, gaunt farmer with a sunburned face that hadn't been shaved in days. 'I saw him! There was nobody else in the dale!'

"He was the farmer who had been working in the field.

"Matthäi stepped forward.

"'People,' he called out, 'I am Inspector Matthäi. We are prepared to hand over the peddler to you!'

"The surprise was so great the crowd became dead silent.

"'Are you out of your mind?' the magistrate hissed at Matthäi.

"'From time immemorial, criminals in our country have been convicted by courts if they are guilty and set free if they are not guilty,' Matthäi continued. 'You have now decided to make yourselves this court. Whether you have the right to do so is something we won't examine here. You have taken that right.'

"Matthäi spoke clearly and distinctly, and the farmers and workers listened attentively. Every word mattered to them. Because Matthäi was taking them seriously, they took him seriously, too.

"'But there is something I must ask of you,' Matthäi continued, 'that I would ask of any other court: justice. For obviously we can only deliver the peddler to you if we are convinced that you want justice.'

34

"'We do!' one man shouted.

"'Your court has to meet one condition if it is to be a just court. That condition is: injustice must be avoided. You have to submit to this condition.'

"'Agreed!' cried a foreman from the brickyard.

"'Therefore you must examine whether the charge of murder against von Gunten is just or unjust. How did the suspicion arise?'

"'The bastard has a record already,' a farmer yelled.

"'That makes von Gunten more suspect,' Matthäi explained, 'but it doesn't prove that he committed the murder.'

"'I saw him in the dale,' the farmer with the tanned, bristly face called out again.

"'Come up here,' the inspector said.

"The farmer hesitated.

"'Go, Heiri,' someone called, 'don't be a coward.'

"The farmer walked up the steps. He looked uncertain. The mayor and the public prosecutor had stepped back into the doorway of The Stag, so that Matthäi stood alone on the top of the stairs with the farmer.

"'What do you want from me?' the farmer asked. 'My name is Heiri Benz.'

"The Mägendorfers stared intently at the two men. The policemen had hung their truncheons back on their belts. They, too, were watching the proceedings breathlessly. The boys of the village had climbed up the half-raised ladder of the fire truck.

"'You watched the peddler von Gunten in the dale, Herr Benz,' the inspector began. 'Was he alone in the dale?'

"'Alone.'

"'What kind of work were you doing, Herr Benz?'

"'I was planting potatoes with my family.'

"'How long had you been doing that?'

"'Since ten o'clock. I also had lunch with my family in the field,' the peasant said.

"'And you observed no one except the peddler?'

"'No one, I swear,' the farmer affirmed.

"'Come on, Benz!' a worker called out. 'I passed your field at two!'

"Two other workers spoke up. They, too, had passed the dale on bicycles at around two.

"'And I drove my cart through the dale, you nitwit,' a farmer shouted. 'But you're always working like a maniac, you miser, and you work your family so hard their backs are all crooked. A hundred naked women could pass you and you wouldn't look up.'

"Laughter.

"'So the peddler wasn't alone in the dale,' Matthäi continued. 'But let's keep searching. There's a road to the city running parallel to the woods. Did anyone take that road?'

"'Fritz Gerber did,' someone called out.

"'I took the road,' a heavyset farmer admitted from his seat on the fire engine.

"'With my cart.'

"'When?'

"'At two.'

"'There's a path leading from that road to the scene of the crime,' the inspector noted. 'Did you notice anyone, Herr Gerber?'

"'No,' the farmer growled.

"'How about a parked car?'

"The farmer looked startled. 'I think so,' he said uncertainly. "'Are you sure?'

"'There was something there.'

"'Maybe a red Mercedes sports car?'

"'Could be.'

"'Or a gray Volkswagen?'

"'That's possible, too.'

"'Your answers are pretty vague,' Matthäi said.

"'Well, I was half-asleep on that cart,' the farmer admitted. 'It happens to everyone in this heat.'

"'Then I'll take this occasion to point out to you that you're not supposed to sleep on a public road,' Matthäi reprimanded him.

"'The horses watch out,' the farmer said.

"Everyone laughed.

"'Now you can see the difficulties you face as judges,' Matthäi said. 'The crime was by no means committed in solitude. Just fifty meters away from the family working in the field. If they had watched out, this awful thing could not have happened. But they were unconcerned, because they hadn't the slightest idea that such a crime was likely to happen. They didn't see the little girl nor the others coming down the road. They noticed the peddler, that's all. But Herr Gerber, too, was dozing on his cart. He can't supply any significant evidence with the necessary exactness. That's where things stand. Does that prove the peddler guilty? You have to ask yourselves that question. One thing that speaks in his favor is that he alarmed the police. I don't know how you intend to proceed as judges, but I want to tell you how we of the police would like to proceed.'

"The inspector paused. Once again he stood alone in front of the Mägendorfers. The embarrassed Benz had returned to the crowd.

"'Every suspect, without regard for his position, would be investigated with the greatest precision. Every conceivable clue would be followed up. Not only that, the police of other countries would be put on the case if that should prove necessary. You see, your court does not have many resources for finding out the truth. We have a huge apparatus at our disposal. Now decide what should be done.'

"Silence. The Mägendorfers had grown thoughtful.

"'Will you really hand him over to us?' the foreman asked.

"'Word of honor,' Matthäi replied. 'If you insist on it.'

"The Mägendorfers were undecided. The inspector's words had made an impression. The public prosecutor was nervous. The situation looked dangerous to him. But then he sighed with relief.

"'Take him with you,' a farmer had yelled.

"Silently, the Mägendorfers formed a lane for the cars. Relieved, the public prosecutor lit himself a Brissago.

"'That was risky, Matthäi,' he said. 'What if you'd been forced to keep your word?'

"'I knew that wouldn't happen,' the inspector calmly replied.

"'Let's hope you never make a promise you can't keep,' the public prosecutor said. He relit his cigar, said good-bye to the mayor, and went back to his car, which was now free to leave.'"

8

"Matthäi did not drive back with the magistrate. He climbed into the van with the peddler. The policemen made room for him. It was hot inside the big car. They didn't dare open the windows yet. Although the Mägendorfers had cleared a space, the farmers were still standing around. Von Gunten cowered behind the driver. Matthäi sat down next to him.

"'I am innocent,' von Gunten said softly.

"'Of course,' Matthäi said.

"'No one believes me,' von Gunten whispered. 'The police don't either.'

"The inspector shook his head. 'You're just imagining that.'

"The peddler was not reassured. 'You don't believe me either, sir.'

"The car started. The policemen sat in silence. Night had fallen outside. The street lamps cast golden lights on the stony faces. Matthäi felt the distrust with which everyone regarded the peddler, the suspicion rising. He felt sorry for him.

"'I believe you, von Gunten,' he said, and noticed that he wasn't quite convinced of that. 'I know you are innocent.'

"The first houses of the city were drawing near.

"'We still have to present you to the chief, von Gunten,' the inspector said. 'You're our most important witness.'

"'I understand,' the peddler murmured, and then he whispered again: 'You don't believe me either.'

"'Nonsense.'

"The peddler insisted. 'I know it,' he said very softly, almost inaudibly, and he stared into the red and green neon-lit advertisements that flashed through the windows of the steadily advancing car like eerie constellations."

9

"Those were the events that were reported to me at headquarters after I had come back from Berne on the seven-thirty express. It was the third infanticide of this kind. Two years earlier, a girl had been killed with a razor in Schwyz canton, and three years before that, another girl in St. Gallen canton. No trace of the perpetrator in either case. I sent for the peddler. The man was forty-eight, short, fleshy, unhealthy, probably a big talker and rather brazen, but now he was frightened. His testimony was clear at first. He had lain down by the edge of the woods, taken off his shoes, put his peddler's basket beside him on the grass. He had intended to go to Mägendorf, where he hoped to sell his brushes, suspenders, razor blades, shoelaces, etc., but on the way he had learned from the mail carrier that Wegmüller was on vacation and that Riesen was substituting for him. So he hesitated and lay down in the grass; he said young policemen are usually prone to fits of efficiency—'I know those guys,' he said. He started to doze off. He described the place: a little dale in the shadow of the woods, with a road running through it. Not far away, a family of farmers on their field, with their dog circling around them. Lunch at The Bear in Fehren had been hefty, he said, a 'Bernese platter' and red wine. He liked to eat well, he said, and he had the means to pay for it. 'I may look ragged, unshaven,

41

and disheveled,' he said, 'but I'm not the way I look, I'm the sort of peddler who earns his living and has some money on the side.' He'd had lots of beer, too, he said, and later, in the grass, two bars of Lindt's chocolate. Eventually the advancing storm with its gusts of warm wind had put him to sleep. But a little later he had the impression that a scream had awakened him, the high scream of a little girl, and staring out into the dale, dazed and still half-asleep, he thought he saw the peasant family on the field lift their heads in surprise for a moment and then return to their stooped positions while their dog continued to circle around them. It must have been some bird, he thought, maybe an owl, how would he know? That explanation reassured him. He dozed on, but then he noticed how deadly quiet the landscape had suddenly become and how the sky had darkened. Thereupon he slipped into his shoes and slung his basket over his back, feeling uneasy and apprehensive as he thought back on that mysterious bird cry. On account of this mood, he decided not to risk a run-in with Riesen and to forget about Mägendorf, which had always been an unprofitable hole anyway. He decided to go back to the city and took the forest path as a shortcut to the train station, whereupon he bumped into the body of the murdered girl. Then he ran to The Stag in Mägendorf and informed Matthäi; he said nothing to the farmers, for fear of being suspected.

"That was his statement. I had the man taken away, but not released. Not quite correct, I suppose, since the public prosecutor hadn't given orders for him to be held, but we didn't have time to be dainty. His story sounded true to me, but it had to be checked, and after all, von Gunten had a record. I was in a bad mood. This case didn't feel right; everything had somehow gone wrong; I didn't know exactly how, but I felt it. I withdrew to my 'boutique,' as I called it, a smoke-filled little room next to my office. I ordered a bottle of Château Neuf du Pape from a restaurant near the Sihl bridge, drank a few glasses. There was always an awful mess in that room, I won't deny it, a jumble of books and files. I did that on principle, because in my opinion it's everyone's duty in this well-ordered land to maintain little islands of chaos, even if only in secret. Then I asked to see the photographs. They were horrible. Then I studied the map. You couldn't have come up with a more perfidious choice of a location. It was theoretically impossible to determine whether the murderer came from Mägendorf, from one of the surrounding villages, or from the city, or whether he had come by foot or by train. Everything was possible.

"Matthäi came.

"'I'm sorry you had such a sad case to deal with on your last day,' I said to him.

"'It's our job, Chief.'

"'When I look at the pictures of this murder, I feel like chucking this damn job,' I said, putting the pictures back in the envelope.

"I was annoyed and perhaps not fully in control of my feelings. Matthäi was my best inspector—you can see how I call him Inspector instead of Lieutenant, it's less correct, but friendlier, somehow. His departure went very much against my grain.

"He seemed to guess my thoughts.

"'I think you had best turn over the case to Henzi,' he said.

"I hesitated. I would have accepted his proposal immediately if this were not a sexually motivated murder. Any other crime is easier to deal with. All you have to do is consider the motives—lack of money, jealousy—and already you've got a circle of suspects and can start closing in from there. But in the case of a sex murder, this method leads nowhere. A guy could be on a business trip, he sees a girl or a boy, he gets out of his car—no witnesses, no observations, and in the evening he's back home, perhaps in Lausanne, perhaps in Basel, anywhere, and there we are, standing around without any clues. I didn't underestimate Henzi; he was a capable public servant, but he didn't have enough experience, in my opinion.

"Matthäi did not share my reservations.

"'He's been working under me for three years,' he said. 'I taught him everything he knows, and I can't imagine a better successor. He'll do the job exactly the way I would. And besides, I'll still be here tomorrow,' he added.

"I sent for Henzi and ordered him to take over the murder department with Officer Treuler. He was delighted; this was his first 'independent case.'

"'Thank Matthäi,' I muttered, and asked him what the mood in the rank and file was like. We were floundering, had nothing to go on, no results, and it was important that the men didn't sense our uncertainty.

"'They're convinced we already have the killer,' Henzi remarked.

"'The peddler?'

44

"'It's not a farfetched suspicion. Von Gunten was already convicted of molesting a minor.'

"'A fourteen-year-old,' Matthäi interjected. 'That's a little different.'

"'We should cross-examine him,' Henzi suggested.

"'That can wait,' I decided. 'I don't believe the man had anything to do with the murder. He's just not very appealing, and that immediately gives rise to suspicion. But that's a subjective reaction, gentlemen, not criminological evidence. It's not the sort of clue we want to rely on.' "With that, I dismissed the two men. My mood did not improve."

10

"We sent out all our available men. That night already and on the following day, we called garages to ask whether traces of blood had been observed in a car, and later we called the laundries. Then we checked all the alibis of everyone who had had a brush with certain paragraphs in the civil code. Near Mägendorf our people scoured the woods with dogs and even with a mine detector, hoping to find tracks and especially the murder weapon. They systematically searched every square meter, climbed into the gorge, searched the brook, collected everything they found there, combed through the woods all the way up to Fehren.

"I, too, took part in the search in Mägendorf, which wasn't my usual way. Matthäi, too, seemed on edge. It was a perfectly pleasant spring day, the air was light, no föhn, but our mood was dark. Henzi interrogated the farmers and factory workers in The Stag, and we set out to visit the school. We took a shortcut and walked straight through a meadow with fruit trees. Some of them were already in full bloom. We could hear the sound of children singing in the schoolhouse: 'Then take my hands and lead me.' The school yard was empty. I knocked on the door of the room where the hymn was being sung, and we stepped in.

"The singers were girls and boys, six to eight years old. The three lowest grades. The teacher who was conducting dropped her hands and looked at us suspiciously. The children stopped singing.

"Fräulein Krumm?'

"Yes?'

"Gritli Moser's teacher?'

"What do you want?'

"Fräulein Krumm was about forty, thin, with large sorrowful eyes.

"I introduced myself and addressed the children.

"Good morning, children!'

"They looked at me with curiosity.

"Good morning!'

"That's a pretty song you were singing.'

"We're practicing a hymn for Gritli's funeral,' the teacher explained.

"In the sandbox stood a model of Robinson Crusoe's island. Children's drawings hung on the walls.

"What sort of child was Gritli?' I asked hesitantly.

"We all loved her,' the teacher said.

"What about her intelligence?'

"She was an extremely imaginative child.'

"Again I hesitated.

"I should ask the children a few questions.'

"Go ahead.'

"I stepped in front of the class. Most of the girls still wore braids and brightly colored aprons.

"I'm sure you have heard what happened to Gritli Moser,' I said. 'I'm the chief of police, which is like a captain in the army. It's my job to find the man who killed Gritli. I want to talk to you now as if you were grown-ups, not children. The man we are looking for is sick. All the men who do such things are sick. And because they are sick, they try to lure children to a hiding place where they can hurt them, a forest or a cellar, any kind of hidden place, and it happens very often. In our canton, we have more than two hundred cases a year. And sometimes it happens that such a man hurts a child so badly that it has to die, like Gritli. That's why we have to lock these men up. They're too dangerous to be allowed to walk around freely. Now, you may ask why we don't lock them up before something bad happens to a child like Gritli? Because there is no way to recognize these sick people. Their sickness is inside, not outside.'

"The children listened breathlessly.

"'You must help me,' I continued. 'We must find the man who killed Gritli Moser, otherwise he will kill another little girl.'

"I was now standing in the midst of the children.

"'Did Gritli tell any of you that a stranger talked to her?'

"The children were silent.

"'Did you notice anything unusual about Gritli recently?'

"The children knew nothing.

"'Did Gritli own anything new recently that she didn't use to have?'

"The children didn't answer.

"'Who was Gritli's best friend?'

"'Me,' a girl whispered.

"She was a tiny little thing with brown hair and brown eyes. 'What's your name?' I asked.

"'Ursula Fehlmann.'

"'So you were Gritli's friend, Ursula.'

"'We sat together.'

"The girl spoke so softly I had to bend down to hear her.

"'And you didn't notice anything either?'

"'No.'

"'Gritli didn't meet anyone?'

"'Someone, yes,' the girl replied.

"'Whom did she meet?'

"'Not a person,' the girl said.

"That answer startled me.

"'What do you mean by that, Ursula?'

"'She met a giant,' the girl said softly.

"'A giant?'

"'Yes,' the girl said.

"'You mean she met a big man?'

"'No, my father is a big man, but he's not a giant.'

"'How big was he?' I asked.

"'Like a mountain,' the girl replied, 'and black all over.'

"'And did this—giant—give Gritli a present?' I asked.

"'Yes,' said the girl.

"'What was it?'

"'Little hedgehogs.'

"'Hedgehogs? What do you mean by that, Ursula?' I asked, completely nonplussed.

"'The whole giant was full of little hedgehogs,' the girl said.

"'But that's nonsense, Ursula,' I objected. 'A giant doesn't have hedgehogs!'

"'He was a hedgehog giant.'

"The girl insisted on her story. I went back to the teacher's desk.

49

"'You're right,' I said. 'Gritli does seem to have had a lot of imagination, Fräulein Krumm.'

"'She was a poetic child,' the teacher replied, turning her sad eyes away from me. 'I should go back to practicing the hymn now. For the burial tomorrow. They're not singing well enough yet.'

"She gave the pitch.

"'Then take my hands and lead me,' the children sang out again."

11

"We went to The Stag, where we relieved Henzi and continued with the questioning of the Mägendorf population. Nothing came of that either, and in the evening we drove back to Zurich no better informed than we had been in the morning. Silently. I had smoked too much and had drunk the local red wine. You know those slightly questionable wines. Matthäi, too, sitting next to me in the back of the car, was in a dark, brooding mood. He didn't start talking until we were almost in Römerhof.

"'I don't believe the killer was a Mägendorfer,' he said. 'It must be the same perpetrator as the one in St. Gallen and Schwyz; those murders were all alike. I think it's probable that the man is operating from Zurich.'

"'Possibly,' I replied.

"'Most likely it's a man with a car, maybe a traveling salesman. That farmer, Gerber, saw a car parked in the woods.'

"'I personally questioned Gerber today,' I said. 'He admitted he was too sound asleep to notice anything.'

"We fell silent again.

"'I'm sorry I have to leave you in the middle of an unresolved case,' he began then, in a somewhat tentative tone of voice, 'but I have that contract with the Jordanian government.'

"'You're flying tomorrow?' I asked.

"'At three P.M.,' he replied. 'Via Athens.'

"'I envy you, Matthäi,' I said, and I meant it. 'I, too, would rather be police chief among the Arabs than here in Zurich.'

"Then I dropped him off at the Hotel Urban, where he had been living as long as I could remember, and went to the Kronenhalle, where I ate under the painting by Miro. That's my regular table. I always sit there and eat 'from the trolley.'"

12

"But when I went back to headquarters around ten and passed by Matthäi's former office, I ran into Henzi in the hallway. He had left Mägendorf at noon already. I had found that rather surprising, but since I had put him in charge of the case, I didn't think it appropriate to criticize him. Henzi was a native of Berne, ambitious, but well liked by the men. He had married a girl from one of the most respectable families in Zurich, had switched from the Socialist party to the Liberals, and was well on his way to making a career for himself. I'm just mentioning this on the side; he's with the Independents now.

"'The bastard still won't confess,' he said.

"'Who?' I asked, very surprised, and stopped in my tracks. 'Who won't confess?'

"'Von Gunten.'

"I didn't know what to think. 'Nonstop?' I asked.

"'All afternoon,' Henzi said, 'and we'll go on through the night if we have to. Treuler's handling him now. I just stepped out for a breather.'

"'I want to have a look at that,' I said—I was curious—and went into Matthäi's former office."

13

"The peddler had taken a seat on a backless office chair. Treuler had moved his chair over to Matthäi's old desk, which served him as a support for his left arm. His legs were crossed and his head was propped on his left hand. He was smoking a cigarette. Feller was taking down the testimony. Henzi and I stood in the doorway, invisible to the peddler, whose back was turned to us.

"'I didn't do it, Officer,' the peddler mumbled.

"'I didn't say you did. I only said you could have done it,' Treuler replied. 'We'll see whether I'm right or not. Let's start from the beginning. So you settled down comfortably by the edge of the woods?'

"'Yes, Officer, that's what I did.'

"'And you slept?'

"'That's right, Officer.'

"'Why, when you were on your way to Mägendorf?'

"'I was tired, Officer.'

"'Then why did you ask the mailman about the policeman in Mägendorf?'

"'To find out, Officer.'

"'To find out what?'

"'My license hadn't been renewed. So I wanted to know how things stood policewise in Mägendorf.'

54

"'And how did things stand policewise?'

"'I found out that there was a substitute in Mägendorf. That scared me, Officer.'

"'I'm a substitute, too,' the policeman dryly declared. 'Are you scared of me, too?'

"'Yes, I am, Officer.'

"'And that's the reason why you didn't want to go to the village?'

"'Yes, Officer.'

"'That's not a bad version of the story,' Treuler said with, it seemed, genuine appreciation. 'But perhaps there is another version which would have the merit of being true.'

"'I have told the truth, Officer.'

"'Weren't you really trying to find out from the mailman whether there was a policeman nearby or not?'

"The peddler looked at Treuler suspiciously. 'What do you mean by that, Officer?'

"'Well,' Treuler replied in a leisurely, unhurried tone, 'you wanted assurance from the mailman that there were no police in that little valley, because you were waiting for the girl, I believe.'

"Horrified, the peddler stared at Treuler. 'Officer, I didn't know the girl,' he cried desperately, 'and even if I had, I couldn't have done it. I wasn't alone there. Those farmers were working in their field. I'm not a murderer. Please believe me!'

"'I do believe you,' Treuler placated him, 'but I have to check your story, you have to understand that. You said that after your nap you went into the woods in order to return to Zurich?'

55

"'There was a storm coming,' the peddler explained, 'so I wanted to take the shortcut, Officer.'

"'And that's when you came across the body?'

"'Yes.'

"'And you never touched the body?'

"'That's right, Officer.'

"Treuler was silent. Even though I couldn't see the peddler's face, I could feel his fear. I felt sorry for him. And yet I was more and more convinced of his guilt, though perhaps only because I wanted badly to find the murderer.

"'We took away your clothes, von Gunten, and gave you other clothes. Can you guess why?'

"'I don't know, Officer.'

"'To make a benzidine test. Do you know what that is, a benzidine test?'

"'No, Officer, I don't,' the peddler weakly replied.

"'A chemical test to find traces of blood,' Treuler declared in an eerily good-natured manner. 'We found blood on your jacket, von Gunten. It's the girl's blood.'

"'Because . . . because I stumbled over the body, Officer,' von Gunten groaned. 'It was horrible.'

"He covered his face with his hands.

"'And of course you concealed this fact from us because you were afraid?'

"'Yes, sir, that's right.'

"'And now we're supposed to believe you again?'

"'I'm not the murderer, Officer,' the peddler pleaded desperately, 'please believe me. Send for Herr Matthäi, he knows I'm telling the truth. Please.'

"'Lieutenant Matthäi has nothing to do with this case any longer,' Treuler replied. 'He's flying to Jordan tomorrow.'

"'To Jordan,' von Gunten whispered. 'I didn't know that.'

"He stared at the floor and fell silent. The room was profoundly still. The only sound was the ticking of the clock. Now and then a car passed by on the street.

"Now Henzi took over. First he closed the window; then he sat down behind Matthäi's desk with a friendly, considerate air, except that he set the table lamp in such a way that its glare shone into the peddler's face.

"'Don't get upset, Herr von Gunten,' the lieutenant said very politely. 'We don't wish to hurt you in any way; we're just trying to find out the truth. That's why we're turning to you. You are the most important witness. You must help us.'

"'Yes, sir,' the peddler replied. He seemed to regain some courage.

"Henzi stuffed his pipe. 'What do you smoke, von Gunten?'

"'Cigarettes, sir.'

"'Give him one, Treuler.'

"The peddler shook his head. He stared at the floor. The light was glaring in his eyes.

"'Is the lamp bothering you?' Henzi asked amiably.

"'It's shining right in my eyes.'

"Henzi changed the position of the shade. 'Is that better?'

"'Better,' von Gunten quietly replied. His voice sounded grateful.

"'Tell me, von Gunten, what sort of objects do you sell? Dishrags?' Henzi began.

57

"'Yes, dishrags, too,' the peddler said hesitantly. He didn't know what the question was leading to.

"'And what else?'

"'Shoelaces, sir. Toothbrushes. Toothpaste. Soap. Shaving cream.'

"'Razor blades?'

"'That, too, sir.'

"'What brand?'

"'Gillette.'

"'Is that all, von Gunten?'

"'I think so, sir.'

"'Fine. But I think you forgot a few things,' Henzi said, and started fussing with his pipe. 'It won't draw,' he said, and then casually continued: 'Go ahead, von Gunten, just list the rest of your little things. We've examined your basket carefully.'

"The peddler was silent.

"'Well?'

"'Kitchen knives, sir,' the peddler said softly and sadly. Beads of sweat gleamed on the back of his neck. Henzi puffed out one cloud of smoke after the other, looking perfectly calm and relaxed, a friendly young gentleman, full of goodwill.

"'Go on, von Gunten, what else, besides kitchen knives?'

"'Straight razors.'

"'Why did you hesitate to admit that?'

"The peddler was silent. Henzi casually stretched out his hand as if to readjust the lampshade. But he removed his hand when von Gunten flinched. The policeman stared fixedly at the peddler, who was smoking one cigarette after another. Henzi's pipe, too, was filling the room with smoke. The air was suffocating. I wanted to open the windows, but keeping them shut was part of the method.

"'The girl was killed with a straight razor,' Henzi said discreetly. It almost sounded like an incidental remark. Silence. The peddler sat slumped, lifeless, in his chair.

"'My dear Herr von Gunten,' Henzi continued, leaning back, 'let's talk man to man. We don't have to pretend to each other. I know that you committed the murder. But I also know that you are just as shocked by the deed as I am, as we all are. It just came over you. You suddenly became like an animal, you attacked the girl and killed her without wanting to, and you couldn't do otherwise. Something was stronger than you.

And when you came back to your senses, von Gunten, you were horrified. You ran to Mägendorf because you wanted to turn yourself in, but then you lost courage. The courage to confess. You must find that courage again, von Gunten. And we want to help you find it.'

"Henzi fell silent. The peddler swayed slightly on his office chair. He seemed about to collapse.

"'I am your friend, von Gunten,' Henzi asserted. 'Take advantage of this opportunity.'

"'I'm tired,' the peddler moaned.

"'So are we all,' Henzi replied. 'Sergeant Treuler, bring us coffee and later some beer. For our guest, too. We play fair here, at the cantonal police.'

"'I am innocent, Inspector,' the peddler whispered hoarsely. 'I am innocent.'

"The telephone rang; Henzi answered, listened attentively, hung up, smiled.

"'Tell me, von Gunten, what was it you had for lunch yesterday?' he asked, as if idly.

"'Bernese platter.'

"'Very nice, and what else?'

"'Cheese for dessert.'

"'Emmentaler, Gruyère?'

"'Tilsiter and Gorgonzola,' von Gunten replied, wiping the sweat from his eyes.

"'Peddlers eat well,' Henzi replied. 'And that's all you ate?'

"'That's all.'

"'I would think that over carefully,' Henzi admonished him.

"'Chocolate,' von Gunten remembered.

"'You see, there was something else,' Henzi said, giving him an encouraging nod. 'Where did you eat it?'

"'By the edge of the woods,' the peddler said, with a tired, mistrustful look at Henzi.

"The lieutenant switched off the desk lamp. Only the ceiling lamp was still weakly shining through the smoke-filled room.

"'I just received the coroner's report, von Gunten,' he declared in a regretful tone. 'They've done the autopsy on the girl. There was chocolate in her stomach.'

"Now I, too, was convinced of the peddler's guilt. His confession was only a question of time. I nodded at Henzi and left the room."

14

"I was not mistaken. The next morning, on a Saturday, Henzi called me at seven. The peddler had confessed. I was in the office at eight. Henzi was still in Matthäi's former office. He was looking out of the open window and turned tiredly to greet me. Beer bottles on the floor, ashtrays overflowing. No one else was in the room.

"'A detailed confession?' I asked.

"'He'll give one later,' Henzi replied. 'The main thing is, he confessed to the murder.'

"'I just hope you stayed within bounds,' I grumbled. The interrogation had lasted over twenty hours. Of course that wasn't legal; but in the police force, you can't always play by the rules.

"'We didn't use any irregular methods, Chief,' Henzi declared.

"I went into my 'boutique' and had the peddler brought in. He could hardly stand on his feet and had to be supported by the policeman who escorted him; but he didn't sit down when I invited him to.

"'Von Gunten,' I said, with an inadvertently friendly note in my voice, 'I hear you have confessed to the murder of little Gritli Moser.'

"'I killed the girl,' the peddler replied so softly that I

61

could hardly hear him, staring at the floor. 'Now leave me in peace.'

"'Get some sleep, von Gunten,' I said, 'we'll talk later.'

"He was led away. In the doorway he encountered Matthäi. The peddler stopped. He was breathing heavily. His mouth opened as though he wanted to say something, but no words came out. He just looked at Matthäi, who seemed faintly discomfited as he stepped aside to make room for him.

"'Go ahead,' the policeman said, and led von Gunten away. "Matthäi stepped into the 'boutique,' closed the door behind him. I lit a Bahianos.

"'Well, Matthäi, what do you think?'

"'The poor guy was questioned for over twenty hours?'

"'That's a method Henzi learned from you. You were always a tenacious interrogator,' I replied. 'But he handled his first independent case nicely, don't you think?'

"Matthäi didn't reply.

"I ordered two coffees and croissants.

"We both had a bad conscience. The hot coffee didn't improve our mood.

"'I have a feeling,' Matthäi finally said, 'that von Gunten will retract his confession.'

"'Could be,' I replied morosely. 'Then we'll just have to work him over again.'

"'You think he's guilty?' he asked.

"'You don't?' I asked in return.

"Matthäi hesitated: 'Well, I suppose I do,' he replied without conviction.

"The morning flooded in through the window. A dull silver. From the Sihlquai came the noises of the street, and the slap of boots as soldiers marched out of their nearby barracks.

"Then Henzi appeared. He stepped in without knocking.

"'Von Gunten has hanged himself,' he reported."

"The cell was at the end of the long corridor. We ran over there. Two men were already busy with the peddler. He was lying on the floor. They had torn open his shirt. His hairy chest was completely immobile. His suspenders still dangled from the window.

"'It's no use,' one of the policemen said. 'The man is dead.'

"I relit my Bahianos, and Henzi lit himself a cigarette.

"'That settles the case of Gritli Moser,' I said as we wearily walked down the endless corridor back to my office. 'As for you, Matthäi—I wish you a pleasant flight to Jordan.'"

"But at two o'clock, when Feller drove to the Hotel Urban for the last time in order to take Matthäi to the airport—the luggage was already in the trunk of the car—the inspector said: 'We've still got some time, let's go by way of Mägendorf.' Feller obeyed and drove through the woods. They reached the village square as the funeral procession drew near, a long line of silent people. A large crowd from the surrounding villages, and from the city as well, had streamed in to attend the funeral. The newspapers had already reported von Gunten's death. There was a general sense of relief. Justice had won. Matthäi and Feller had left the car and were now standing among children opposite the church. The coffin lay on a bier on top of a cart drawn by two horses, and was surrounded by white roses. Behind the coffin followed the children of the village, two by two, each pair with a wreath, led by Fräulein Krumm, the principal, and the pastor, the girls dressed in white. Then two black figures, the parents of Gritli Moser. The woman stopped and looked at the inspector. Her face was expressionless, her eyes were empty.

"'You kept your promise,' she said very quietly, but with such precision that the inspector heard it. 'I thank you.' Then she walked on. Unbowed, proud beside a broken husband who had suddenly become an old man.

"The inspector waited until the whole procession had passed by—the mayor, government officials, farmers, workers, housewives, daughters, all in their finest, most solemn dress. No one spoke a word. The spectators, too, were perfectly still. All you could hear in the glow of the afternoon sun was the pealing of churchbells, the rumbling sound of the cart wheels, and the countless footsteps on the hard pavement of the village street.

"'To the airport,' Matthäi said, and they got back into the car."

17

"After he had taken leave of Feller and walked through the passport control, he bought a *Neue Zürcher Zeitung* in the waiting room. There was a picture of von Gunten in it, with a caption describing him as the murderer of Gritli Moser, but there was also a picture of the inspector with an article about his appointment to serve the kingdom of Jordan. A man at the pinnacle of his career. But when he stepped onto the runway, his raincoat over his arm, he noticed that the terrace of the building was full of children. Several school classes had come to visit the airport—girls and boys in colorful summer clothes. There was much waving of little flags and handkerchiefs, whoops of amazement as the giant silver machines descended and took off. The inspector halted, then walked on toward the waiting Swissair plane. When he reached it, the other passengers were already aboard. The stewardess who had led the travelers to the plane held out her hand to receive Matthäi's ticket, but the inspector turned around once more. He looked at the crowd of children, who were waving, happily and enviously, at the plane which was about to start.

"'Miss,' he said, 'I'm not flying,' and returned to the airport building, and walked under the terrace with its vast crowds of children, through the building and on toward the exit."

18

"I didn't receive Matthäi until Sunday morning—not in the 'boutique,' but in my official office with its equally official view of the Sihlquai. Pictures by Gubler, Morgenthaler, Hunziker on the walls, all reputable Zurich painters. I was in a bad mood on account of a disagreeable call from a man of the political department who insisted on speaking French and French only; the Jordanian embassy had lodged a protest, and the Federal Council had requested information which I was in no position to give, since I did not understand my former subordinate's action.

"'Sit down, Herr Matthäi,' I said. I suppose the formality of my manner saddened him. We sat down. I did not smoke, and gave no indication that I intended to. That disturbed him. 'The federal government,' I said, 'concluded a treaty with Jordan concerning the transfer of a police expert to their department. And you, too, Herr Matthäi, signed a contract with Jordan. Due to your failure to depart, these contractual agreements have been violated. We both have had legal training. I don't need to make myself plainer.'

"'That's not necessary,' Matthäi said.

"'I therefore ask you to go to Jordan as quickly as possible,' I suggested.

"'I'm not going,' Matthäi retorted.

"'Why not?'

"'Gritli Moser's murderer hasn't been found yet.'

"'You think the peddler was innocent?'

"'Yes, I do.'

"'We have his confession.'

"'He must have lost his nerve. The long interrogation, the despair, the feeling of being abandoned. And I'm not without blame in this matter,' he quietly continued. 'The peddler turned to me and I didn't help him. I wanted to go to Jordan.'

"The situation was peculiar. Just the day before, we had conversed in a relaxed, collegial manner, and now we were sitting face-to-face, stiff and formal, both of us in our Sunday clothes.

"'I request that you put me back in charge of the case, Chief,' Matthäi said.

"'I can't do that,' I replied. 'Not under any circumstances; you are no longer with us, Herr Matthäi.'

"The inspector stared at me in surprise.

"'I'm dismissed?'

"'You resigned from the cantonal police service when you agreed to accept a position in Jordan,' I quietly replied. 'Now you've broken your contract. That's your affair. But if we employ you again it would mean that we condone your action. I'm sure you'll understand that this is impossible.'

"'I see,' Matthäi said. 'I understand.'

"'Unfortunately, there's nothing to be done about it,' I decided.

"For a while we were both silent.

"'Driving through Mägendorf,' Matthäi said softly, 'on my way to the airport, there were children there.'

"'What do you mean by that?'

"'In the funeral procession, lots of children.'

"'That's not surprising,' I said.

"'And at the airport there were children, too, whole classes from various schools.'

"'So?' I was mildly bewildered.

"'Assuming I'm right, assuming the murderer of Gritli Moser is still alive and free, wouldn't other children be in danger?' Matthäi asked.

"'Certainly,' I calmly replied.

"'If the possibility of such a danger exists,' Matthäi continued with urgent emphasis, 'it is the duty of the police to protect the children and prevent another crime.'

"'So that's why you didn't take that flight,' I asked slowly, 'to protect the children?'

"'That's why,' Matthäi replied.

"'I said nothing for a while. I saw the whole thing more clearly now and was beginning to understand Matthäi.

"'The possibility that children are in danger has to be accepted,' I said then. 'If you are right, we can only hope that the real killer will reveal himself at some point or, at worst, leave some clues after his next crime. It may sound cynical, what I'm saying, but it isn't. It's just terrible. The power of the police has limits and has to have limits. Everything is possible, even the most improbable things are possible, but we have to go by what's probable. We can't say with certainty that von Gunten was guilty; guilt is never established with certainty; but we can say that von Gunten was probably guilty. If we don't want to invent an unknown perpetrator, the peddler is the only serious candidate. He had a previous conviction for sexual molestation, he carried around razors and chocolate, he had blood on his clothes, and besides, he plied his trade in Schwyz and St. Gallen, where the other two murders happened. And in addition, he gave a confession and committed suicide. To doubt his guilt at this point is simply amateurish. Common sense tells us that von Gunten was the murderer. Yes, common sense can be wrong, we're only human—but that's a risk we have to take. And unfortunately, the killing of Gritli Moser is not the only crime we have to deal with. We just sent the emergency squad out to Schlieren. And last night we had four major burglaries. From a purely technical point of view, we can't afford the luxury of reopening that case. We can only do what is possible, and we have done that. Children are always endangered. There are about two hundred cases of sexual assault on children each year. In our canton alone. We can educate the parents, warn the children, and we've done all that. But we can't weave the nets of police surveillance so tightly that no crimes ever happen. Crimes always happen, not because there aren't enough policemen, but because there are policemen at all. If *we* weren't needed, there wouldn't be any crimes. Let's keep that in mind. We have to do our duty, you're right about that, but our first duty is to stay within our limits, otherwise we'll end up with a police state.'

"I fell silent.

"Outside, the church bells started to ring.

"'I can understand that your personal—situation—has become difficult. You've fallen between two chairs,' I said politely by way of conclusion.

71

"'I thank you, sir,' Matthäi said. 'For the time being, I'll be looking into the case of Gritli Moser. Privately.'

"'I suggest you give up on this matter,' I said.

"'I have no intention of doing that,' he replied.

"I didn't show my irritation.

"'May I request, in that case, that you not bother us with this anymore,' I said, standing up.

"'As you wish,' Matthäi said. Whereupon we said good-bye without shaking hands."

19

"It was hard for Matthäi to walk past his former office and leave the empty police headquarters. The nameplate on his door had already been changed, and when he ran into Feller, who sometimes hung around the office on Sundays, the man was embarrassed, and barely murmured a greeting. Matthäi felt like a ghost, but what bothered him more was that he no longer had an official car at his disposal. He was determined to return to Mägendorf as quickly as possible, but this resolve was not so easy to carry out. The village was nearby, but the trip was complicated. He had to take the number eight streetcar and transfer to the bus. In the streetcar he met Treuler, who was on his way with his wife to visit her parents. Treuler stared at the inspector, obviously surprised, but asked no questions. And then other acquaintances crossed Matthäi's path, among them a professor of the Technical College and an artist. He evaded their questions about his reasons for not leaving. It was an embarrassing situation each time, because his 'promotion' and departure had already been celebrated. He felt like a specter, like a man resurrected from the dead.

"The church bells had stopped ringing in Mägendorf. The farmers were standing on the village square in their Sunday clothes or going into The Stag in small groups. The air had become cooler. Mighty cloud banks were wandering in from the west. In the Moosbach dale, the boys were already playing soccer; there was nothing to suggest that a crime had been committed near the village. Everyone was cheerful. Somewhere people were singing 'Am Brunnen vor dem Tore.' In front of a large farmhouse with half-timbered walls and a mighty roof, children were playing hide-and-seek; a boy counted up to ten with a loud voice, and the others hurried away. Matthäi watched them.

"'Man,' a soft voice next to him said. He looked around.

"Between a pile of logs and a garden wall stood a little girl in a blue skirt. Brown eyes, brown hair. Ursula Fehlmann.

"'What do you want?' asked the inspector.

"'Stand in front of me,' the girl whispered, 'so they won't find me.'

"The inspector stood in front of the girl.

"'Ursula,' he said.

"'You mustn't talk so loud,' the girl whispered. 'They'll hear that you're talking to someone.'

"'Ursula,' the inspector whispered. 'I don't believe what you said about the giant.'

"'What don't you believe?'

"'That Gritli Moser met a giant who was as big as a mountain.'

"'But there is a giant.'

"'Have you seen one?'

"'No, but Gritli did. Be quiet now.'

"A red-haired boy with freckles came slinking around the corner of the house. He was the seeker. He stopped in front

74

of the inspector, then tiptoed around the other side of the farmhouse. The girl giggled quietly.

"'He didn't notice me.'

"'Gritli told you a fairy tale,' the inspector whispered.

"'No,' said the girl, 'every week the giant waited for Gritli and gave her hedgehogs.'

"'Where?'

"'In Rotkehler Dale,' Ursula answered. 'And she made a picture of him. So he has to exist. And the little hedgehogs, too.'

"Matthäi was startled.

"'She drew the giant?'

"'The drawing's on the wall in the classroom,' the girl said. 'Step aside.' And already she had squeezed through the pile of logs and Matthäi, leaped toward the farmhouse, and with a jubilant cry touched the doorjamb before the boy who came hurrying out from behind the house could tag her."

20

"The news I received on Monday morning was strange and disturbing. First the mayor of Mägendorf called to complain that Matthäi had broken into the schoolhouse and stolen a drawing by the murdered Gritli Moser; he said he wouldn't stand for any more prying by the cantonal police in his village, that the people needed to calm down after the horrors they'd been through; and he concluded with a not very politely phrased promise to personally chase Matthäi out of town with a dog if he ever showed up again. Then Henzi complained about an extremely awkward run-in with Matthäi, right in the middle of the Kronenhalle, where his former boss, already noticeably drunk, had guzzled a whole bottle of Réserve du Patron, followed that up with a cognac, and accused Henzi of 'judicial murder.' Henzi's wife, the former Fräulein Hottinger, had been revolted by the display. But that wasn't all. After the morning report, Feller told me that some character from the city police— of all the embarrassing witnesses—had reported to him that Matthäi had been sighted in various bars and was now staying at the Hotel Rex. I also learned that Matthäi had started smoking. Parisiennes. It was as if the man was transformed, metamorphosed, as if he had changed his character overnight. It all sounded like an impending nervous breakdown. I called a psychiatrist whose expert opinion we often consulted.

"To my surprise, the doctor said that Matthäi had made an appointment with him for the afternoon; whereupon I informed him of what had happened.

"Then I wrote a letter to the Jordanian embassy. I told them Matthäi was ill and asked them to grant him a two-month leave, after which, I said, the inspector would come to Amman."

21

"The private clinic was far out of town, near the village of Röthen. Matthäi had taken the train and had to walk a considerable stretch. He had been too impatient to wait for the mail truck. Now it passed him, and he gazed after it with irritation. He walked through several small hamlets. Children were playing by the roadside, and the farmers were working in the fields. The sky was overcast, silvery. The weather had turned cold again; the temperature was sliding toward the freezing point, fortunately without quite reaching it. Matthäi wandered along the edge of the hills and after passing Röthen turned into the path that led across the plain to the clinic. The first thing that met his eye was a yellow building with a tall chimney, some gloomy old factory, perhaps. But soon the scene became more appealing. The main building was still hidden by beeches and poplars, but he also noticed cedars and a huge sequoia. He entered the grounds of the clinic. The path forked. Matthäi followed a sign: *Office*. He saw a pond gleaming through the trees and shrubs, but perhaps it was only fog. Dead silence. Matthäi heard nothing but his steps crunching on the gravel. Later he heard a rasping sound. A young man was raking the path with slow and regular movements. Matthäi halted irresolutely. He looked about for a new sign; he didn't know where to turn.

"'Can you tell me where the office is?' he asked the young man. He received no answer. The fellow kept raking, in a steady, regular motion, like a machine, as if no one had spoken to him, as if he were alone. His face was expressionless, and since he appeared to be very strong—an impression that was accentuated by the lightness of his labor—the inspector felt vaguely threatened. As though the man might suddenly strike out at him with his rake. He walked on hesitantly and entered a courtyard. This led to a second, larger yard with colonnades on both sides, rather like a cloister; but the third side was bounded by a building that appeared to be a country house. Again there was no one in sight, though he could hear a plaintive voice, high and pleading, repeating a single word again and again, without cease. Again Matthäi paused doubtfully. An inexplicable sadness befell him. Never had he felt so discouraged. He pressed down the latch of an old portal full of deep cracks and carved graffiti; but the door did not yield. The voice kept lamenting, over and over. Like a somnambulist he walked down the colonnade. There were red tulips in some of the stone vases, yellow ones in others. But now he heard steps; a tall, elderly, dignified gentleman crossed the yard, looking displeased and faintly surprised. A nurse was leading him.

"'Hello,' the inspector said. 'I'm looking for Dr. Locher.'

"'Do you have an appointment?' the nurse asked.

"'I'm expected.'

"'Just go to the salon,' the nurse said, pointing to a double door. 'Someone will come for you.' Then she walked on, arm in arm with the old man, who appeared to be in a daze, opened a door, and disappeared with him. The voice was still crying out its litany. Matthäi entered the salon. It was a large room with antique furniture, large easy chairs, and an enormous sofa. Above it, in a heavy golden frame, hung the portrait of a man, probably the founder of the hospital. There were other pictures on the walls, tropical landscapes. Matthäi thought he recognized the outskirts of Rio de Janeiro. He went to another double door. It opened out onto a terrace. Large cacti stood on the stone parapet. But he could no longer oversee the grounds; the fog had thickened. Vaguely, Matthäi could make out a wide expanse of land with some tomb or monument on it, and the menacing, shadowy form of a silver poplar. The inspector was getting impatient. He lit a cigarette; his new addiction calmed him. He went back to the room, to the sofa. In front of it stood an old round table with old books: Gustav Bonnier, *Flore complète de France, Suisse et Belgie.* He turned its pages; meticulous drawings of flowers, grasses—beautiful, no doubt, and calming, but they meant nothing to the inspector. He smoked another cigarette. Finally a nurse came, a small energetic person with rimless glasses.

"'Herr Matthäi?' she asked.

"'Certainly.'

"The nurse looked around. 'Don't you have any luggage?'

"Matthäi shook his head. The question surprised him for a moment.

"'I just want to ask the doctor a few questions,' he replied.

"'Follow me, please,' the nurse said, and led him through a low door."

22

"He entered a small and, to his surprise, rather humbly furnished room. Nothing about it suggested a doctor's office. On the walls were pictures similar to the ones in the salon, as well as photographs of serious men with rimless glasses and beards, monstrous faces. Predecessors, no doubt. The desk and the chairs were loaded with books; only an old leather armchair remained unoccupied. The doctor, in a white coat, sat behind his files. He was small, lean, birdlike, and wore rimless glasses, like the nurse and the bearded men on the wall. Rimless glasses, it seemed, were obligatory here, and maybe, Matthäi thought, they were the insignia of some secret order, like the tonsure of monks.

"The nurse withdrew. Locher rose and greeted Matthäi.

"'Welcome,' he said, looking faintly embarrassed, 'make yourself comfortable. It's a little shabby in here. We're a charitable institution, so we're always short of money.'

"Matthäi sat down in the leather armchair. It was so dark in the room that the doctor had to switch on the desk lamp.

"'May I smoke?' Matthäi asked.

"Locher seemed taken aback. 'Certainly,' he said, observing Matthäi attentively over the top of his dusty glasses. 'But you didn't used to smoke, did you?'

"'Never.'

"The doctor took out a sheet of paper and started to scribble on it—some kind of note, apparently. Matthäi waited.

"'You were born on November eleventh, 1903, am I right?' the doctor asked, writing as he spoke.

"'That's right.'

"'Still in the Hotel Urban?'

"'It's the Rex now.'

"'Oh, it's the Rex now. In the Weinbergstrasse. So you're still living in hotel rooms, my dear Matthäi?'

"'That seems to surprise you?'

"The doctor looked up from his papers.

"'Look, man,' he said, 'you've been living in Zurich for thirty years now. Other people establish families, produce offspring, build for the future. Do you have any private life at all? Excuse my asking so directly.'

"'I understand,' Matthäi replied. He suddenly understood everything, including the nurse's question about his luggage.

'The chief gave you a report.'

"The doctor carefully put aside his fountain pen. 'What do you mean by that, sir?'

"'You've been assigned to examine me,' Matthäi said, crushing out his cigarette. 'Because in the eyes of the cantonal police I am not quite—normal.'

"The two men fell silent. Outside the fog hovered in front of the window, a dull, faceless twilight that crept into the little room full of books and stacks of files. The air was chilly and stale, mixed with the smell of some sort of medicine.

"Matthäi rose, went to the door, and opened it. Outside stood two men in white smocks, their arms folded. Matthäi closed the door again.

"'Two attendants. In case I cause problems.'

"Locher remained unperturbed.

"'Listen, Matthäi,' he said. 'I will now speak to you as a doctor.'

"'As you wish,' Matthäi replied, and sat down.

"'I have been informed,' Locher said, picking up his fountain pen, 'that you have recently committed acts that can no longer be called normal. So a few frank words are in order. You have a tough job, Inspector, and I'm sure you have to be tough with the people who come into your sphere. You'll have to forgive me for speaking so frankly: my profession, too, has made a tough man of me, and a suspicious one. When I consider your behavior, I find it peculiar that you should all of a sudden drop a once-in-a-lifetime chance like this Jordanian assignment. Then this fixed idea of having to search for a murderer who has already been found. Next, this sudden decision to smoke, and this equally sudden compulsion to drink. Four double cognacs after a bottle of Réserve! I'm sorry, my friend, that looks an awful lot like an abrupt personality change, like the symptoms of an incipient illness. It would be only to your advantage to have yourself thoroughly examined so we can clarify the picture, clinically as well as psychologically. Which is why I suggest that you spend a few days in Röthen.'

"The doctor fell silent and returned to scribbling on his sheet of paper.

"'Do you have occasional fevers?'

"'No.'

"'Speech problems?'

"'No.'

"'Voices?'

"'Nonsense.'

"'Sudden perspiration?'

"Matthäi shook his head. The deepening dusk and the doctor's talk were making him impatient. He groped for his cigarettes, found them at last, and as he took the burning match the doctor handed him, he noticed his fingers were trembling. With anger. The situation was too silly; he should have foreseen this and chosen another psychiatrist. But he had a special affection for this doctor, who was consulted at headquarters more to do him a favor than because of his expertise; he trusted him because other doctors spoke disparagingly of his abilities, because he was considered an eccentric.

"'Agitated,' the doctor noted, almost with pleasure. 'Shall I call the nurse? If you'd like your room . . .'

"'Absolutely not,' Matthäi replied. 'Do you have any cognac?'

"'I'll give you a sedative,' the doctor suggested, standing up.

"'I don't need a sedative, I need cognac,' the inspector roughly replied.

"The doctor must have pushed a hidden button, for an attendant appeared in the doorway.

"'Bring a bottle of cognac and two glasses from my apartment,' the doctor ordered, rubbing his hands, presumably because they were cold. 'And hop to it.'

84

"The attendant left.

"'Really, Matthäi,' the doctor said, 'it's urgent that you sign yourself in. Unless you want a major physical and mental breakdown. We do want to avoid that, don't we? And I think we can, with a little finesse.'

"Matthäi did not reply. The doctor, too, remained silent. The telephone rang. Locher took the receiver and said: 'I can't talk now.' The darkness outside was almost black now. Evening had fallen with extraordinary suddenness.

"'Shall I switch on the ceiling light?' the doctor asked, merely for the sake of saying something.

"'No.'

"Matthäi had regained his composure. When the attendant came with the cognac, he poured himself a glass, drank it, filled it again.

"'Locher,' he said, 'why don't you drop this idiotic man-to-man and hop-to-it talk. Look: you are a doctor. Have you in your profession ever been confronted with a case you couldn't solve?'

"The doctor looked at Matthäi with astonishment. The question unsettled him. He couldn't imagine why it was being asked.

"'Most of my cases can't be solved,' he finally, honestly, replied, although at the same time he sensed that he should never have given this reply to a patient.

"'That doesn't surprise me, given the nature of your profession,' Matthäi replied with an irony that saddened the doctor.

"'Did you come here only to ask me this question?'

"'Among other things.'

"'For God's sake, what is your problem?' the doctor asked, feeling acutely uneasy. 'You used to be reason personified.'

"'I don't know,' Matthäi replied uncertainly. 'The murdered girl.'

"'Gritli Moser?'

"'I can't stop thinking about that little girl.'

"'You can't get her off your mind?'

"'Do you have children?' Matthäi asked.

"'I'm not married either,' the doctor replied softly, again ill at ease.

"'So you're not either.' Matthäi brooded silently. 'You see, Locher,' he explained then, 'I looked and took in what I saw; I didn't turn my eyes away like my successor, Henzi, Mr. Normal. There was a mutilated corpse lying on the leaves. Only the face was untouched, a child's face. I stared at her red skirt in the bushes, at the pieces of pretzel strewn around. But that wasn't the terrible thing.'

"Matthäi fell silent again. As if frightened. He was a man who never spoke of himself and was now forced to do so, because only this little birdlike doctor with the ridiculous eyeglasses could help him, and in exchange for that help, he had to confide in him.

"'You rightly wondered,' he finally continued, 'that I'm still living in a hotel. I didn't want to confront the world. I wanted to deal with it skillfully, I'd almost say mechanically, but I didn't want to suffer with it. I wanted to be superior to it, not lose my head, control it all like a technician. I looked at the murdered girl, and that was bearable; but when I stood in front of her parents, I suddenly couldn't bear it any longer, I had to get away from that godforsaken house, and so I promised by my eternal soul that I would find the murderer—just to turn my back on those suffering people, and I never gave a moment's thought to the fact that I couldn't keep this promise because I was going to Jordan. And then I allowed the old indifference to rise up in me, Locher. That was so horrible. I didn't fight for the peddler. I allowed everything to take its course. I became my old impersonal self, "Dead-end Matthäi," as I'm called in certain parts of town. I slipped back into the calm, the superiority, the formality, the inhumanity, until I saw the children at the airport.'

"The doctor pushed away his notes.

"'I turned back,' Matthäi said. 'You know the rest.'

"'And now?' the doctor asked.

"'And now I am here. Because I don't believe the peddler was guilty, and now I have to keep my promise.'

"The doctor rose and went to the window.

"The attendant came in, followed by his colleague.

"'Go to the ward,' said the doctor. 'I don't need you anymore.'

"Matthäi poured himself another cognac, laughed.

"'Good, this Rémy Martin.'

"The doctor still stood by the window, staring out.

"'How can I assist you?' he asked dejectedly. 'I'm not a criminologist.' Then he turned to face Matthäi. 'Why do you believe the peddler was innocent?' he asked.

"'Here.'

"Matthäi put a piece of paper on the table and carefully unfolded it. It was a child's drawing. At the lower right, in clumsy script, was the name 'Gritli Moser.' It was a crayon drawing of a man. He was big, bigger than the pines that surrounded him like strange stalks of grass. The face was drawn in a child's manner—two dots, a comma, a dash, and a circle. He was wearing a black hat and black clothes, and from his right hand, which was a round disk with five lines, several small disks with many little hairlines, like stars, fell onto a tiny little girl who was even smaller than the pines. On the very top of the page—in the sky, actually—stood a black automobile, and next to it a peculiar animal with strange horns.

"'This drawing was made by Gritli Moser,' Matthäi explained. 'I got it from the schoolroom.'

"'What is it supposed to represent?' the doctor asked, staring at the drawing in bewilderment.

"'The hedgehog giant.'

"'What's that supposed to mean?'

"'Gritli said a giant had given her little hedgehogs in the woods. The drawing is about that encounter,' Matthäi explained, pointing to the little disks.

"'And now you believe . . .'

"'It's not unreasonable to suppose that Gritli Moser's hedgehog giant was her murderer, and that this is a picture of him.'

"'Nonsense, Matthäi,' the doctor retorted with irritation. 'This drawing is a pure product of the imagination. I'm sorry to disappoint you.'

"'Probably it is,' Matthäi replied. 'But the car is too well observed for that. I'd even say it's an old American model. And the giant has a lifelike quality, too.'

"'But there's no such thing as a giant,' the doctor said impatiently. 'Don't tell me any fairy tales.'

"'A tall, massively built man could look like a giant to a little girl.'

"The doctor looked at Matthäi with surprise.

"'You think the murderer was a big man?'

"'That's just a vague assumption,' the inspector said evasively. 'If I'm right, the murderer is driving around in an old black American car.'

"Locher pushed his glasses up to his forehead. He took the drawing into his hand and examined it closely.

"'So what am I supposed to do?' he asked uncertainly.

"'Assuming that all I knew about the murderer was that this drawing represented him,' Matthäi said, 'then this would be my only clue. But in that case I would be in the position of a layman confronted with an X-ray photograph. I wouldn't know how to interpret the drawing.'

"The doctor shook his head.

"'There is nothing we can infer about the murderer from this drawing,' he replied, putting the sheet of paper back on the table. 'At best, it's possible to make a judgment about the girl who drew it. She must have been intelligent, bright, and cheerful. You see, children don't just draw what they see, they also draw what they feel about what they see. Fantasy and reality are mixed together. So some things on this drawing are real—the big man, the car, the girl; other elements seem to be in some kind of code—the hedgehogs, the animal with the large horns. These are all riddles. And the solution to these riddles—well, I'm afraid Gritli took the answer with her to the grave. I am a doctor, not a spiritualist medium. Pack up your drawing. It makes no sense to go on thinking about it.'

"'You're afraid.'

"'I hate to waste my time.'

"'What you call a waste of time may just be an old method,' Matthäi declared. 'You're a scientist, you know what a working hypothesis is. My assumption that this is a picture of the murderer is a working hypothesis. I am asking you to make believe with me. Let's see what comes of it.'

"Locher looked at the inspector thoughtfully for a moment and then examined the drawing once more.

"'What did the peddler look like?' he asked.

"'Inconspicuous.'

"'Intelligent?'

"'Not stupid, but lazy.'

"'Wasn't he convicted of a sex crime once?'

"'He got involved with a fourteen-year-old.'

"'Relations with other females?'

"'Well, as a peddler, yes. He was known to chase skirts all over the place,' Matthäi replied.

"Now Locher was interested. Something didn't sound right.

"'Too bad this Don Juan confessed and hanged himself,' he grumbled, 'because he doesn't sound like a sex maniac at all. But let's adopt your hypothesis. The hedgehog giant on the drawing—I could imagine him being a sex fiend. He looks big and massive. People who commit these kinds of crimes against children are usually primitive, more or less feebleminded, imbeciles, mental defectives, as we say in the profession, robust, tending toward violence, and hampered by impotence or inferiority complexes with regard to women.'

"He stopped and peered more closely at the drawing.

"'Strange,' he said.

"'What?'

"'The date underneath the drawing.'

"'Well?'

"'More than a week before the murder. Gritli Moser must have met her murderer before, presuming your hypothesis is correct, Matthäi. It seems peculiar, though, that she would tell the story of her encounter in the form of a fairy tale.'

"'It's a child's way.'

"Locher shook his head. 'People don't do things without a reason, and that goes for children as well,' he said. 'Probably the big black man forbade Gritli to tell anyone about their mysterious meeting. And the poor girl obeyed him and told a fairy tale instead of the truth. Otherwise someone would have become suspicious and she might have been saved. I have to say that in this case the story becomes downright ghoulish. Was the girl raped?' he suddenly asked.

"'No,' Matthäi replied.

"'And the same thing happened to the girls who were killed years ago in St. Gallen and Schwyz?'

"'Exactly.'

"'Also with a razor?'

"'The same.'

"Now the doctor also poured himself a cognac.

"'This is not a sex crime,' he said. 'It's an act of revenge. These murders were supposed to wreak some kind of revenge against women—regardless now of who did it, the peddler or poor Gritli's hedgehog giant.'

"'But a little girl is not a woman.'

"Locher continued undeterred. 'No, but to a sick man, she could replace a woman,' he said. 'Since the murderer is afraid of approaching women, he plucks up his courage when he sees a little girl. He kills her in place of the woman. That's why he will always approach the same sort of girl. Look at your records, you'll find that the victims are all alike. Don't forget that this is a primitive person. It doesn't matter whether the feeblemindedness is inborn or due to an illness—such people have no control over their instinctual drives. Their ability to resist their impulses is abnormally weak. It takes very little— an altered metabolism, a few degenerated cells—and such a person becomes a beast.'

"'And the reason for his revenge?'

"The doctor considered the question. 'Maybe sexual conflicts,' he explained. 'Perhaps the man was oppressed or exploited by a woman. Maybe his wife was rich and he was poor. Maybe she occupied a higher social position than he did.'

"'None of that applies to the peddler,' Matthäi said.

"The doctor shrugged.

"'Then something else will apply. Every kind of absurdity is possible between a man and a woman.'

"'Is there a continuing danger of new murders?' Matthäi asked. 'Assuming the murderer isn't the peddler.'

"'When did the murder in St. Gallen happen?'

"'Five years ago.'

"'And the one in Schwyz?'

"'Two years ago.'

"'The intervals are getting smaller,' the doctor noted. 'That could indicate an accelerated psychological deterioration. Apparently the sick man's resistance to affects is weakening, and he would probably commit another murder in a few months, perhaps even weeks, if an opportunity presents itself.'

"'And how would he behave in the meantime?'

"'At first he would feel something like relief,' the doctor said a little hesitantly, 'but soon new feelings of hatred would start building up, and a new need for revenge would make itself felt. He would start loitering in places where there are children—in front of schools, for instance, or in public squares. Then he would gradually move on to driving about in his car in search of a new victim. And once he found the girl, he would befriend her, until eventually it would happen again.'

"Locher fell silent.

"Matthäi took the drawing, folded it, and put it in his breast pocket. Then he stared at the window. It was night outside.

"'Wish me luck in finding the hedgehog giant, Locher,' he said.

"Startled, the doctor looked at him. Suddenly he understood: 'This hedgehog giant is more than just a working hypothesis for you, isn't it, Matthäi?'

"Matthäi admitted it. 'For me, he is real. I don't doubt for a moment that he is the murderer.'

"'But everything I told you was mere speculation,' the doctor explained. 'I was just toying around with ideas; there's no scientific value in that!' The doctor was irritated. How could he have allowed himself to be tricked like that? He had realized too late what Matthäi's intentions were.

"'I was just pointing out one of a thousand other possibilities,' he continued. 'With this method, you could prove anyone guilty of killing that child. Why not? Any absurdity can be imagined and somehow logically supported, and you know that very well. I went along with your hypothesis just to be friendly and helpful, but please, be man enough now to look at reality without hypothetical ifs and maybes, and have the courage to accept the factors that plainly prove the peddler's guilt. That drawing is just a product of a child's imagination, or else it corresponds to her meeting with some person other than the murderer, someone who couldn't possibly be the murderer.'

"'You can safely leave it to me,' Matthäi replied as he finished his glass of cognac, 'to determine the degree of probability that can be assigned to your deductions.'

"The doctor did not reply immediately. He was sitting behind his old desk again, surrounded by his books and files, worn out by the daily effort to keep afloat the antiquated and poorly equipped hospital whose director he was. 'Matthäi,' he said finally, by way of conclusion, and his voice sounded weary and bitter, 'you are trying to do the impossible. I don't want to get carried away, but this is what I feel: you have your will, your ambition, your pride, you don't like to give up. I understand that, I'm the same way. But when you set out to find a murderer who in all probability doesn't exist, and whom you would not find even if he did exist, because there are too many of his kind who just by chance haven't killed

94

anyone—then things start getting ticklish. You're choosing madness as a method, and it takes courage to do that, no question; extreme positions impress people generally these days; but if this method does not lead to its goal, I'm afraid that in the end, all you'll be left with is the madness.'

"'Farewell, Dr. Locher,' Matthäi said."

23

"This conversation was reported to me by Locher. As usual, his Gothic script, minute and precise as if engraved, was almost illegible. I sent for Henzi. He, too, had a hard time reading the document. His comment was that the doctor himself was calling Matthäi's hypotheses untenable. I wasn't so sure; it seemed to me that the doctor just lacked the courage to stand by his own convictions. I had doubts after all. The peddler had left us no detailed confession, just a general statement concerning his guilt in the crime. Nor had the murder weapon been found. None of the razors found in the basket showed traces of blood. Naturally, this did not clear von Gunten; our original grounds for suspecting him still weighed heavily against him. But I felt uneasy. And Matthäi's actions made more sense to me than I cared to admit. To the investigating magistrate's annoyance I went so far as to have the woods near Mägendorf searched again. Nothing came of that either. The murder weapon was not to be found. Apparently it still lay at the bottom of the gorge, as Henzi believed.

"'Well,' he said, pulling one of his awful perfumed cigarettes from the box, 'that's all we can do about this case for the moment. Either Matthäi is crazy or we are. We have to make up our minds.'

"I pointed to the photographs I had ordered. The three murdered girls resembled each other.

"'That does seem to point to the hedgehog giant,' I said.

"'Why?' Henzi replied cold-bloodedly. 'All it means is that the girls were the peddler's type.' Then he laughed. 'I just wonder what Matthäi's up to. I wouldn't like to be inside his skin.'

"'Don't underestimate him,' I muttered. 'He's capable of anything.'

"'Is he capable of finding a murderer who doesn't exist, Chief?'

"'Perhaps,' I replied, putting the three photographs back among my files. 'All I know is that Matthäi doesn't give up.'

"As it turned out, I was right. The first report came from the chief of the municipal police. After a meeting. We had just settled one of those cases of incompetence that comes up from time to time, when, in the middle of saying good-bye, this bumbler brings up Matthäi. I guess to annoy me. He said Matthäi had been seen at the zoo a number of times, and that he had bought himself an old Nash at a garage on Escher-Wyss Square. Shortly after that, I received another report. This one completely confused me. It was in the Kronenhalle, on a Saturday evening, I remember it exactly. The place was full—everyone who was anybody in Zurich and interested in a good meal was there. Waitresses scurrying around, the food on the trolley steaming, and the rumble of traffic sounding in from the street. I was sitting under the Miró, all unsuspecting, eating my liver dumpling soup, when the sales representative of one of the big fuel companies came up to me, said hello,

97

and sat down at my table, just like that. He was slightly drunk and in high spirits, ordered a marc, and told me, laughing, that my former first lieutenant had changed his profession; that he had taken over a gas station in Graubünden, near Chur—a business the company had been intending to close down, because it had never brought in any profits.

"At first I refused to believe him. The story seemed incongruous, silly, absurd.

"The salesman insisted that what he was saying was true. He praised Matthäi for the way he was handling the job. The gas station was flourishing. Matthäi had many customers. Almost exclusively people he had had dealings with in the past, although in a different capacity. The news must have spread that 'Dead-end Matthäi' had been promoted to gas-station attendant, so all the 'old-timers' were pulling up and zooming in on whatever wheels they had, from the most antediluvian jalopies to brand-new Mercedes. Matthäi's gas station, he said, had become a mecca for the underworld of all eastern Switzerland. Sales were soaring. The company had just installed a second pump for premium gasoline. They had also offered to build him a modern house instead of the shack he was living in. He turned down the offer with thanks, refused to hire an assistant, too. Often there'd be long lines of cars and motorcycles, but everyone was patient. Apparently the honor of having a former first lieutenant of the cantonal police fill your tank was worth a lot.

"I didn't know what to say. The salesman said good-bye, and when the trolley came steaming along I had lost my appetite, just nibbled a little, ordered beer. Later Henzi came, as usual, together with his former Fräulein Hottinger, in a foul mood because the results of some referendum didn't accord with his wishes. I told him the news. He said: 'That proves it, I always predicted Matthäi would go out of his mind, and now it's happened.' He was suddenly in the best of spirits, ate two steaks, while his wife kept talking about some show where she knew some of the actors.

"A few days later, the phone rang. During a meeting. With the municipal police again, naturally. It was the director of an orphanage. The old lady told me in great excitement that Matthäi had appeared at her door, solemnly dressed in black, evidently in order to impress her with his seriousness, and asked her whether he might adopt a certain girl from among her 'charges,' as she put it. It had to be that particular child; he had always wanted a child, he said, and now that he was running a garage in Graubünden by himself, he was in a position to raise one. Naturally she had rejected his request, politely referring to the statutes of the orphanage; but my former first lieutenant made such a peculiar impression on her that she considered it her duty to inform me. Then she hung up. Now, this was indeed a strange state of affairs. I drew on my Bahianos, completely bewildered. But what made Matthäi's behavior impossible for us at headquarters was an entirely different affair. We had arrested a highly question-able character, an unofficial pimp and official hairdresser who had set himself up in a handsome villa by the edge of a lake in a village favored by many poets. At any rate, traffic in that direction got pretty lively—taxis and private cars, every-thing. Now, no sooner had I started questioning him than he popped out with an answer I didn't expect, beaming with pleasure as he rubbed the news under our noses. Matthäi, he said, was shacking up with the Heller girl in his gas station. I immediately called the police in Chur; the story was true. I was dumbstruck. The hairdresser sat gloating in front of my desk, chewing his gum. I gave up. I gave orders to let the old sinner go in the name of God. He had outplayed us.

"The situation was alarming. I was perplexed, Henzi was outraged, the examining magistrate disgusted, and when the federal councillor heard about it, he used the word 'disgrace.' Lotte Heller had once been our guest at headquarters. A colleague of hers—a lady well known all over the city—had been murdered. We suspected that Heller knew more than she was telling us, and eventually she was summarily expelled from the canton of Zurich, even though, apart from her profession, there was no evidence against her. But there are always people in the administration who have their prejudices and feel the need to act on them.

"I decided it was time to intervene, to drive out there. I sensed that Matthäi's actions had something to do with Gritli Moser, but I couldn't imagine how. My ignorance infuriated me; it also made me unsure of myself. But aside from that, I felt a detective's curiosity. As a law-and-order man, I wanted to know what was going on."

24

"I set out in my car, alone. It was a Sunday again, and it seems to me, looking back, that many of the crucial moments in this story took place on Sundays. Bells ringing all around, the whole country seemed to be clanging and chiming; and somewhere in Schwyz canton I got held up by a procession. One car after another on the road, and on the radio, one sermon after the other. Later the sounds of guns banging, whistling, clattering, booming away in shooting booths in every village. A monstrous, senseless commotion—the whole of eastern Switzerland seemed to be on the move; somewhere an automobile race was being held, and droves of cars came rolling in from the west, whole families, clans. It was the noisiest day of rest I had ever experienced. By the time I reached the gas station—the one you saw earlier—I was exhausted. I looked around. The place wasn't as run-down as it is today. It looked friendly, everything clean, geraniums in the windows. There was no tavern yet. The whole thing had a solid, reliable, lower middle-class look about it. There were various objects, too, alongside the street, that indicated the presence of a child: a swing, a large dollhouse on a bench, a doll's carriage, a rocking horse. Matthäi himself was just attending a customer who hastily took off in his Volkswagen as I stepped out of my

Opel. Next to Matthäi stood a seven- or eight-year-old girl with a doll tucked under one arm. She had blond braids and was wearing a red skirt. She looked familiar, but I couldn't remember where I had seen her; she didn't resemble Lotte Heller at all.

"'That was Red Meier, wasn't it?' I said, pointing at the Volkswagen as it moved away. 'He was let out a year ago.'

"'Regular?' Matthäi asked indifferently. He was dressed in a pair of blue mechanic's overalls.

"'Super.'

"Matthäi filled the tank, washed the windshield.

"'Fourteen-thirty.'

"I gave him fifteen. 'Keep the change,' I said. Then I blushed. 'Excuse me, Matthäi, that just slipped out.'

"'That's all right,' he said, slipping the bills in his pocket. 'I'm used to it.'

"Embarrassed, I looked at the little girl again.

"'Cute little thing,' I said.

"Matthäi opened the door of my car. 'I wish you a pleasant ride.'

"'Come on, now,' I muttered. 'I'm really here to talk to you. For Pete's sake, Matthäi, what's all this about?'

"'I promised not to bother you any more with the Gritli Moser case, Chief. Now I must ask you to do the same for me,' he replied, and turned his back on me.

"'Matthäi,' I said, 'let's stop fooling around.'

"He said nothing. I heard some loud popping and whistling nearby, probably another shooting booth. It was shortly before eleven. I watched him attend to an Alfa-Romeo.

"'He served three and a half years,' I said as the car took off. 'Can't we go inside? All this shooting makes me nervous. I can't take it.'

"He led me into the house. In the hallway we met with Lotte Heller. She was coming up from the cellar with potatoes. She was still an attractive woman, and as a policeman I was a little embarrassed—a bad conscience. She gave us a quizzical look, a little disturbed, it seemed, but then she gave me a friendly greeting. She made an altogether good impression.

"'Is that her child?' I asked, after she had left the kitchen.

"Matthäi nodded.

"'Where did you find her?' I asked. 'Lotte Heller, I mean.'

"'Near here. She was working in the brickyard.'

"'And why is she here?'

"'Well,' Matthäi said, 'someone has to do the housework.'

"I shook my head.

"'I need to talk to you in private,' I said.

"'Annemarie, go to the kitchen,' Matthäi said.

"The little girl went out.

"The room was poorly furnished but clean. We sat down at a table by the window. A series of loud bangs erupted outside, one salvo after the other.

"'Matthäi,' I said, 'what's this all about?'

"'Very simple, Chief,' my former first lieutenant replied. 'I'm fishing.'

"'What do you mean?'

"'Detective work, Chief.'

"Annoyed, I lit a Bahianos.

"'I'm not a beginner, but I still don't understand.'

"'Let me have one of those.'

"'Help yourself,' I said, shoving the box over to his side. "Matthäi put a bottle of kirsch on the table. We were sitting in the sun; the window was half-open. Outside, the geraniums, mild June weather, and banging guns. Whenever a car stopped—which happened more rarely now, since it was around noon—Lotte Heller worked the pump.

"'You got Locher's report on our conversation,' Matthäi said after carefully lighting the Bahianos.

"'That didn't get us anywhere.'

"'But it did me.'

"'How so?' I asked.

"'The child's drawing reflects the truth.'

"'I see. And what are those hedgehogs?'

"'That I don't know yet,' Matthäi replied, 'but I do know what that beast with the strange horns was supposed to be.'

"'Well?'

"'It's an ibex,' Matthäi said, with a leisurely draw at his cigar. Then he puffed the smoke into the room.

"'That's why you went to the zoo?'

"'For days,' he replied. 'I also had children draw ibexes. Their versions are like Gritli Moser's.' I understood.

"'The ibex is the emblem of Graubünden,' I said. 'It's the old heraldic beast of this region.'

"Matthäi nodded. 'It appears on the license plates issued here. It caught Gritli's eye.'

"The solution was simple.

"'We should have thought of that right away,' I muttered.

"Matthäi watched the ash growing on his cigar, the faint curling of the smoke.

"'The mistake we all made,' he said, 'you, Henzi, and I, was to presume that the killer was operating from Zurich. He's actually from Graubünden. I checked the scenes of the other murders—they're all on the route from Graubünden to Zurich.'

"I reflected on that.

"'Matthäi, there may be something to that,' I had to admit.

"'There's more.'

"'Well?'

"'I met some anglers.'

"'Anglers?'

"'Well, boys who were fishing.'

"I didn't know what to make of that.

"'You see,' he said, 'the first thing I did after my discovery was drive out to the Graubünden canton. Logical. But I soon realized how pointless it was. Graubünden canton is so big—how are you going to find a man about whom you only know that he's big and that he drives a black American car? More than seven thousand square kilometers, more than a hundred and thirty thousand people scattered around countless valleys—it's simply impossible. So there I was, at the end of my tether. One cold day, then, I was sitting by the Inn River, in the Engadine, watching some boys by the water. I was about to turn away when I noticed that the boys had become aware of me. They looked frightened, as if put on the spot. One of them was holding a homemade fishing rod. "Go ahead and fish," I said. The boys eyed me suspiciously. "Are you from the police?" one of them asked, a redhead with freckles. "Is that what I look like?" I replied. "Well, I don't know," the boy said. "I'm not from the police," I said. Then I watched them toss the bait into the water. There were five boys, all absorbed in their activity. "No bites," the freckled boy finally said with a resigned shrug, and climbed up the bank to where I was sitting. "Do you have a cigarette?" he asked. "At your age?" I replied with amusement. "You look as if you'd give me one," the boy declared. "In that case, I'll have to," I replied, and held out my pack of Parisiennes. "Thanks," the boy said, "I've got my own matches." Then he blew out the smoke through his nose. "That sure feels good after a total bust with the fishes," he said grandly. "Well," I said, "your friends aren't giving up as quickly as you are. I bet they'll catch something soon." "They won't," the boy said. "Or at most a grayling." "I guess you'd prefer a pike," I teased him. "I'm not interested in pike," the boy replied. "Trout. But that's a question of money." "How come?" I wondered. "When I was a kid, I used to catch them by hand," I said. He shook his head disparagingly. "Those were young ones. Just try and catch a full-grown trout with your hand. They're predators, just like pike, but they're harder to catch. And you need a license, and," the boy added, "a license costs money." "Well, you and your buddies are doing it without money." I laughed. "But the disadvantage," the boy said, "is that we can't get to the right places. That's where the guys with the licenses are." "What's a right place?" I asked. "You obviously don't know a thing about fishing," the boy noted. "I'll admit that," I said. We had both sat down on the embankment. "You think you just drop your bait any old place and wait?" he said. I thought about that and finally said: "What's wrong with that?" "Typical beginner," the freckled boy said, blowing smoke out through his nose again: "To get anywhere with fishing, you have to have two things before anything else: the right place and the right bait." I listened attentively. "Let's say you want to catch a trout," the boy continued, "and I mean one that's full-grown. Remember, the trout needs prey, he's a predator. The first thing you have to figure out is where the fish likes to be. Naturally that would be a place that's protected against the current, but near a strong current, because that's where a lot of animals come swimming along. So I'm talking about a place downstream behind a big rock, or even better, downstream behind a bridgehead. And unfortunately those places are booked by the guys with the licenses." "The stream has to be blocked," I said. "You got it," he said proudly. "And the bait?" I asked. "Well, that depends on what you're after, a predator, or a grayling, or a burbot, which are vegetarians," he replied. "A burbot you can catch with a cherry. But for a predator like a trout or a bass you need something that's alive. A mosquito, a worm, or a little fish." "Something alive," I said thoughtfully, and stood up. "Here," I said, giving the boy the whole packet of Parisiennes. "You've earned these. Now I know how to catch my fish. First I have to find the place and then the bait."'

"Matthäi fell silent. For a long time I said nothing, drank my schnapps, stared out into the lovely late spring day, listened to the rifles popping, and relit my cigar.

"'Matthäi,' I finally said, 'now I understand what you meant by fishing before. This gas station is the propitious spot, and the road is the river, right?'

"Matthäi's face was impassive.

"'Whoever wants to get from Graubünden to Zurich has to use this road,' he quietly replied. 'Otherwise he has to go out of his way through the Oberalp Pass,' he quietly replied.

"'And the girl is the bait,' I said. My own words frightened me.

"'Her name is Annemarie,' Matthäi replied.

"'And now I know who she reminds me of,' I said. 'Gritli Moser.'

"We both fell silent again. It had grown warmer outside; the mountains were shimmering in the haze, and the shooting continued. There must have been some kind of contest.

"'Isn't that a rather devilish scheme?' I finally asked hesitantly.

"'Possibly,' he said.

"'You intend to wait here until the murderer comes along, sees Annemarie, and falls into the trap you laid out for him?'

"'The murderer *has* to come by here,' he replied.

"I thought about that. 'All right,' I said then, 'let's assume you're right. This murderer exists. Obviously, it's possible. Anything's possible in our profession. But don't you think your method is too risky?'

"'There is no other way,' he declared, and threw his cigarette butt out the window. 'I know nothing about the murderer. I can't search for him. So I had to search for his next victim, a girl, and use the child as a bait.'

"'Fine,' I said, 'but you adapted this method from the art of fishing. Those are two different worlds. You can't keep a little girl near the road as bait all the time. She

108

has to go to school, she'll want to get away from your damn highway.'

"'Summer vacation's coming,' Matthäi replied stubbornly.

"I shook my head.

"'I'm afraid you're getting obsessed,' I replied. 'You can't just stay here waiting for something you think should happen that may not happen at all. It's true, the murderer probably does pass through here, but that doesn't mean he'll reach for your bait—to use your comparison. And then you'll be waiting and waiting....'

"'Anglers have to wait, too,' Matthäi replied stubbornly.

"I gazed out the window, watched the woman filling up Oberholzer's tank. Six years in Regensdorf jail altogether.

"'Does Lotte Heller know why you're here, Matthäi?'

"'No,' he replied. 'I told the woman I needed a housekeeper.'

"I felt very uneasy. The man impressed me; his method was certainly unusual, in fact there was something magnificent about it. I suddenly admired him, and wished him success, if only to humiliate that awful Henzi; but still I considered his undertaking to be hopeless, the risk too great, the chances of winning too small.

"'Matthäi,' I said, trying to reason with him, 'there's still time for you to assume that post in Jordan. If you don't, the guys in Berne will send Schafroth.'

"'Let him go.'

"I still wouldn't give up. 'Wouldn't you like to join us again?'

"'No.'

"'We would have you work in the office for the time being, at your old salary.'

"'Don't feel like it.'

"'You could switch to the municipal police. Consider that just from a financial point of view.'

"'At this point I'm almost making more money here than I did working for the state,' Matthäi replied. 'But here's a new customer, and Fraulein Heller is probably busy preparing her roast.'

"He stood up and walked out. Then another customer arrived. Pretty-boy Leo. When Matthäi was done with him, I was already in my car.

"'Matthäi,' I said as I took leave, 'you're really beyond help.'

"'That's the way it is,' he replied, and signaled to me that the road was clear. Next to him stood the girl in the red skirt, and in the doorway stood Lotte Heller, wearing an apron, looking extremely mistrustful. I drove home."

25

"So he waited. Relentlessly, obstinately, passionately. He served his customers, did his work—pumping gas, checking the fluids, washing the windshields, always the same mechanical operations. The child was always next to him or playing with her dollhouse when she came back from school, skipping, hopping, watching the goings-on with wondering eyes, talking to herself; or else she would sit on the swing in her red skirt, singing, pigtails flying. He waited and waited. The cars drove past him, cars of all colors and price ranges, old cars, new cars. He waited. He wrote down the license plates of vehicles from Graubünden canton, looked up their owners in the records, called the town registrars to inquire about them. Lotte Heller worked in a small factory near the village up toward the mountains, and would come back in the evening down the little incline behind the house, with her shopping bag and a net full of bread. Sometimes at night they heard footsteps around the house, and low whistles, but she never opened the door. Summer came, a shimmering, heavy, endless heat that frequently discharged its tension with thunderous downpours, and finally the schools closed and the long summer vacation began. Matthäi's chance had come. Annemarie was now always with him by the edge of the road and thus always visible to everyone who drove past. He waited and waited. He played with the girl, told her fairy tales, the whole Brothers Grimm, all of Andersen, *A Thousand and One Nights*, invented some stories of his own, desperately did everything he could to attach the girl to himself and to the road where he needed her to be. The child stayed, content with the stories and fairy tales. The drivers regarded the pair with wonderment or were touched by this idyll of father and child, gave the girl chocolate, chatted with her, while Matthäi lurked and watched, waiting for his moment. Was that big heavy man the killer? His car had Graubünden plates. Or that long tall thin one who was talking to the girl now? Owner of a candy store in Disentis, as Matthäi had found out long ago. 'Want your oil checked? As you wish. I'll fill your tank. That'll be twenty-three ten. Have a pleasant trip, sir.'

"He waited and waited. Annemarie loved him, was content with him; he had only one thing in mind, the arrival of the killer. Nothing existed for him but this faith, this hope that he would arrive. He longed for no other fulfillment. He imagined how the fellow would look when he came—powerful, clumsy, childlike, trusting, and full of bloodlust; how he would keep coming back with a friendly grin, in his Sunday suit, a retired railroad man or customs official; how she would gradually respond to his luring advances, how Matthäi would follow them to the woods behind the station, treading softly, ducking low, and how at the crucial moment he would leap out, how they would fight then, man to man, a wild, bloody battle, then the deciding blow, the final resolution, the murderer lying before him, beaten to a pulp, whining, confessing. But then he had to admit to himself that all this was impossible because he was

112

much too obviously keeping an eye on the child, that he would have to allow her more freedom if he wanted to see results. Then he allowed Annemarie to wander away from the street but secretly followed her, leaving the gas station unattended, while the cars angrily honked their horns. The girl would skip off to the village, a half hour away, and play with other children near the farmhouses or by the edge of the woods, but always she would come back after a short time. She was used to solitude, and she was shy. And the other children avoided her. Then Matthäi changed his tactics again. He invented new games, new fairy tales, to draw Annemarie back to his side. He waited and waited. With unswerving, unbending resolution. And without explanation. For Annemarie's mother had long since noticed how much attention he gave the child. She had never believed that Matthäi had hired her as a housekeeper out of pure kindness. She sensed that he had some ulterior motive, but she felt safe with him, perhaps for the first time in her life, and so she gave it no further thought. Perhaps she was hopeful of further developments; who knows what goes on in a poor woman's mind. In any case, after a while she ascribed Matthäi's interest in her daughter to genuine affection, although from time to time her old distrust and her old realism returned.

"'Herr Matthäi,' she said once, 'this may be none of my business, but did the chief of the cantonal police come here on my account?'

"'Of course not,' Matthäi said. 'Why would he?'

"'People in the village are talking about us.'

"'Who cares?'

"'Herr Matthäi,' she began again, 'is your being here in some way connected with Annemarie?'

"'Nonsense.' He laughed. 'I just love her, that's all, Fraülein Heller.'

"'You're good to me and Annemarie,' she replied. 'I wish I knew why.'

"Then the summer vacation was over; fall came, the landscape turned red and yellow, everything sharply contoured as if under a huge magnifying glass. Matthäi felt as if a great opportunity had slipped away; but still he waited. Tenaciously, stubbornly. The child walked to school. Matthäi usually went to meet her at noon and in the evening, driving her home in his car. His plan was looking more and more senseless, impossible; his chances of winning were getting slimmer and slimmer, and he knew it. He wondered how often the murderer had driven past his gas station. Maybe every day. Certainly once a week. And yet nothing had happened. He was still groping in the dark, without a clue, without even a hunch; just drivers coming and going, occasionally chatting with the girl in a harmless, casual manner, nothing to pin a suspicion on. Which one of them was the one he was looking for? Was he one of them at all? Perhaps the reason he wasn't succeeding was that too many people knew about his old profession; here was an obstacle he hadn't reckoned with, though it couldn't have been avoided. But still he persevered, waited and waited. He could no longer turn back; waiting was the only method, even though it was wearing him out, even though there were times when he was ready to pack his bags and go anywhere, even to Jordan, just to get away, and other times when he was afraid of losing his mind. Then there were hours, days, when he became indifferent, apathetic, cynical, and let things take their course, sat on the bench in front of the gas station drinking one schnapps after the other, staring into space, littering the ground with cigarette butts. Then he would pull himself together again. But more and more he would sink into apathy, dozing away the days and weeks in a perpetual round of cruel, absurd waiting. But one day as he sat there, unshaven, weary, grease-stained, he was startled by the realization that Annemarie wasn't back from school yet. He set out to meet her, on foot. The unpaved, dusty country road rose slightly behind the house, then dipped down, crossing a barren plain and leading through the woods, from the edge of which one could see the village from afar, old houses huddled around a church, blue smoke over the chimneys. From here one could also see the whole stretch of road down which Annemarie had to come, but there was no sign of her. Matthäi turned back to the forest, suddenly tense and wide-awake; low fir trees, bushes, rustling red and brown leaves on the ground, a woodpecker hammering somewhere in the background where larger fir trees blocked the sky except for slanting shafts of light that broke through their branches. Matthäi left the road, forced his way through briers and undergrowth; branches struck him in the face. He reached a clearing, turned around in surprise; he had never seen it before. From the opposite side, a wide path cut through the woods and ended in the clearing; evidently this was a road used to cart refuse out of the village, for a mountain of ashes was heaped up in the clearing. Along its edges lay tin cans, rusty wires, and similar junk, a regular garbage collection sloping down to a little brook that was bubbling through the middle of the clearing. Only then did Matthäi notice the girl. She was sitting by the bank of the silvery stream with her doll and her school bag beside her.

"'Annemarie,' Matthäi called.

"'I'm coming,' the girl replied, but she remained sitting where she was.

"Matthäi carefully climbed across the garbage and finally stood next to the child.

"'What are you doing here?' he asked.

"'Waiting.'

"'For what?'

"'For the wizard.'

"The girl had nothing but fairy tales in her head; one day she'd be waiting for an elf, the next it would be a wizard; it was like a mockery of his own waiting. Despair overcame him again, the realization of the futility of his actions, and the paralyzing knowledge that he had no choice but to go on waiting because there was nothing left for him to do but wait, wait, and wait.

"'Come on,' he said listlessly, took the child by the hand and walked back with her through the forest, sat down on the bench again, stared into space; twilight came, night; he had become indifferent to everything; he sat there, smoking, waiting and waiting, mechanically, with fixed determination, relentlessly. Once in a while he unconsciously whispered, as if to summon his enemy out of the night: 'Come already, come, come, come.' Then he sat motionless in the white moonlight, and suddenly fell asleep. He woke up stiff and frozen at dawn and crawled into bed.

"But the next morning, Annemarie came home from school earlier than usual. Matthäi had just risen from his bench to pick her up when she came walking along with her school bag on her back, singing quietly and hopping from one foot to another. The doll dangled from her hand, its little feet dragging on the ground.

"'Homework?' Matthäi asked.

"Annemarie shook her head and continued her song: 'Maria sat upon a stone,' and went into the house. He let her go; he was too desperate, too hopeless, too tired to tell new fairy tales, to entice her with new games.

"But when Lotte Heller came home, she asked: 'Was Annemarie a good girl?'

"'What do you mean? She was in school all day,' Matthäi replied.

"Lotte looked at him with surprise: 'In school? But she had the day off, teachers' conference or something.'

"Matthäi sat up straight. The disappointment of the past few weeks was suddenly dispelled. He sensed that the fulfillment of his hopes, of his mad expectation, was near. He controlled himself with difficulty. He asked no more questions of Lotte Heller. Nor did he probe the little girl. But the next afternoon he drove to the village and left the car in a side street. He wanted to watch the girl secretly. It was almost four. From the windows came singing, then screams and shouts, the children poured out of the building, boys were fighting and throwing stones, girls were walking arm in arm; but Annemarie was not among them. The teacher came out and subjected Matthäi to a moment of stern, stiff scrutiny before informing him that Annemarie had not been in school. 'Is she ill?' she asked. 'She was already absent day before yesterday, in the afternoon, and she brought no excuse.' Matthäi replied that the child was indeed sick, said good-bye, and drove like a madman back to the woods. He rushed through the under-brush to the clearing, found nothing. Exhausted, breathing heavily, scratched and bleeding from the thorns, he returned to the car and drove home. But before he reached the gas station, he saw the girl skipping along the edge of the road. He stopped.

"'Get in, Annemarie,' he said pleasantly, after opening the door.

"Matthäi held out his hand to help the girl climb into the car. Then he noticed that her hand was sticky. And when he looked at his own hand, he saw traces of chocolate.

"'Who gave you the chocolate?' he asked.

"'A girl,' Annemarie replied.

"'In school?'

"Annemarie nodded. Matthäi said nothing. He pulled up in front of the house. Annemarie climbed out and sat down on the bench in front of the gas station. Matthäi watched her unobtrusively. The child put something in her mouth and started chewing. Slowly he went up to her.

"'Show me,' he said, and carefully opened the slightly clenched little hand, revealing a prickly brown ball, partly bitten off. A chocolate truffle.

"'Do you have any more?' Matthäi asked.

"The girl shook her head.

"The inspector reached into the pocket of Annemarie's skirt, pulled out her handkerchief, unfolded it, and found two more truffles in it.

"Annemarie was silent.

"Nor did the inspector speak. An enormous happiness had swept over him. He sat down on the bench next to the child.

"'Annemarie,' he finally asked, and his voice was quivering as he carefully held the prickly chocolate balls in his hand, 'did the wizard give them to you?'

"The girl said nothing.

"'Did he forbid you to tell anyone about you and him?' he asked.

"No answer.

"'You're right not to tell,' Matthäi said kindly. 'He's a nice wizard. You can go see him again tomorrow.'

"All at once the girl beamed as if in tremendous joy, embraced Matthäi, ardent with happiness, and ran up to her room."

26

"The next morning at eight—I had just arrived at my office—Matthäi laid the chocolate truffles on my desk. He was so excited that he hardly greeted me. He was wearing his former suit, but without a tie, and he was unshaven. He took a cigar from the box I offered him and started puffing away.

"'What's this chocolate about?' I asked, dumbfounded.

"'The hedgehogs,' Matthäi replied.

"I looked at him, still baffled, turning the little chocolate balls between my fingers. 'What do you mean?'

"'Very simple,' he explained. 'The murderer gave Gritli Moser chocolate truffles, and she turned them into hedgehogs. That's the secret of her drawing.'

"I laughed: 'How do you want to prove that?'

"'Well, the same thing has happened to Annemarie,' Matthäi replied, and gave me a complete report.

"I was instantly convinced. I summoned Henzi, Feller, and four policemen, gave them instructions, and informed the public prosecutor. Then we drove off. The gas station was abandoned. Lotte Heller had taken the child to school and gone on to the factory.

"'Does her mother know what happened?' I asked.

"Matthäi shook his head. 'She has no idea.'

"We went to the clearing. We searched it carefully but found nothing. Then we split up. It was close to noon; Matthäi returned to the gas station in order not to arouse suspicion. It was a favorable day, a Thursday, when the child had no school in the afternoon. Gritli Moser had also been killed on a Thursday—the realization shot through me. It was a bright autumn day, hot, dry, dense with the humming of bees, wasps, and other insects, and with the screeching of birds. From far away, you could hear the echoing blows of an ax. At two o'clock, the bells of the village rang out sharply, and then the girl appeared, broke through the shrubs across from me, effortlessly hopping, jumping, ran to the little brook with her doll, sat down, and gazed steadily toward the woods, attentive, tense, with shining eyes. She seemed to be waiting for someone, but she couldn't see us. We were hidden behind trees and shrubs. Then Matthäi cautiously came back and leaned against a treetrunk near me, as I was doing.

"'I think he'll be here within a half hour,' he whispered.

"I nodded.

"Everything had been meticulously organized. We were keeping an eye on the access road from the highway to the woods. We even had wireless equipment. We were all armed with revolvers. The child was sitting by the brook, almost motionless, full of wondrous, anxious, marveling expectation, the garbage heap at her back. At times she was in the sun, then in the shadow of one of the great dark firs; not a sound could be heard other than the humming of the insects and the trilling of the birds. Now and then the girl sang to herself with her thin voice: 'Maria sat upon a stone,' over and over, always the same words and verses; and heaped around the stone on which she sat were rusty tin cans, metal barrels, and wires; and sometimes abrupt gusts of wind came blowing across the clearing, rousing the leaves till they danced and rustled, until it was quiet again. We waited. Nothing was left of the world but this forest, enchanted by the colors of autumn, and the little girl with her red skirt in the clearing. We waited for the murderer, determined, avid for justice, retribution, punishment. The half hour had long since passed—two whole hours, in fact. We waited and waited; we ourselves now were waiting as Matthäi had waited for weeks and months. Five o'clock came; the first shadows, then the twilight, the dimming, the dulling of all the radiant colors. The girl skipped away. Not one of us said a word, not even Henzi.

"'We'll come back tomorrow,' I decided. 'We'll spend the night in Chur. At the Hotel Steinbock.'

"And so we waited on Friday and Saturday also. I really ought to have used the Graubünden police. But this was our affair. I didn't want to have explain anything, didn't want any interference. The public prosecutor called on Thursday evening already, objected, protested, threatened, dismissed the whole thing as nonsense, flew into a rage, insisted we come back to Zurich. I remained firm, told him we would stay regardless of his objections, and compromised only to the degree of sending one officer back. We waited and waited. At this point we were no longer concerned about the child or the murderer; we were concerned with Matthäi. The man had to be proven right, had to reach his goal, otherwise there would be a disaster; we all felt it, even Henzi, who said he was convinced now. On Friday night he declared firmly that the unknown killer would be coming on Saturday; after all, he said, we had incontrovertible evidence—the hedgehogs—and besides, why would the girl keep coming back to sit in the same spot again and again? She had to be waiting for someone. And so we stood in our hiding places, behind our trees and shrubs, motionless, for hours, staring at the child, at the tin cans, at the tangles of wire, at the mountain of ashes, smoking in silence, never exchanging a word, listening to her perpetual singsong: 'Maria sat upon a stone.' On Sunday the situation was more difficult. The woods were suddenly full of hikers, on account of the long spell of sunny weather. Some sort of mixed chorus with a conductor broke into the clearing, noisy, sweating, shirtsleeved, took up formal positions, and burst into mighty praise of the joys of wandering and the eternal glory of God on high. Thank heaven we weren't in uniform behind our shrubs. Later a couple came along and behaved rather shamelessly despite the presence of the child, who simply sat there, waiting with incomprehensible patience, in rapt anticipation, for the fourth afternoon in a row. We waited and waited. By now the three policemen had gone back with their wireless equipment. There were only four of us left: Henzi, Feller, Matthäi, and I. Strictly speaking our stakeout was no longer justifiable, but Henzi pointed out that Sunday wasn't a safe day for the killer, so the day didn't really count. He was right about that, so we waited on Monday, too. On Tuesday, Henzi went back to headquarters—somebody had to take care of business—but he was still convinced that we were on the verge of finding the murderer.

We waited and waited and waited, constantly hiding, each of us independent of the others now, since we were too few to organize a cordon. Feller had posted himself near the forest path behind a bush, where he lay in the shadow, dozing in the summery heat of that placid autumn and suddenly snoring so intensely that the wind wafted the sounds across the clearing; this happened on Wednesday. Matthäi was standing on the side of the clearing nearest to the gas station, and I was watching the scene from the opposite side. And so we waited in ambush for the murderer, the hedgehog giant, with the child between us, and were startled each time a car passed on the main road. Every day the girl came to the clearing by the little brook, singing 'Maria sat upon a stone,' stubbornly, mindlessly. It was incomprehensible; we began to detest her, hate her. Sometimes, of course, she took a long time to come. She would wander about near the village with her doll, staying clear of the houses, since she was playing hooky. That caused us some problems. I had to talk to her teacher in private to prevent the school from looking into the matter. I cautiously hinted at our reason for being there, identified myself, and obtained her somewhat hesitant consent. Then the child circled the forest. We followed her with our binoculars, but she always returned to the clearing—except for Thursday, when, to our despair, she stayed near the gas station. Whether we wanted to or not, we had to hope for Friday. Now I had to make a decision; Matthäi had long since fallen silent, and was standing behind his tree the next day when the girl came skipping along again with her red dress and her doll and sat down as she had on previous days. The glorious fall weather was still strong, radiant, bursting with life before the long sleep of decay; but the public prosecutor couldn't take another half hour of this. He came at five P.M., in the car with Henzi, showed up completely unexpectedly, came over to me, who had been standing there since one o'clock, constantly shifting from foot to foot, staring at that child, red in the face, I'm sure, with anger at that ceaseless little voice: 'Maria sat upon a stone.' I was so sick of that song, and sick of that child, too, that horrible little gap-toothed mouth, those skimpy braids, that shoddy little red dress; she looked disgusting to me, vulgar, idiotic—I could have strangled her, killed her, torn her limb from limb, just to shut her up and put an end to that awful song. It was maddening. Everything was still as it always had been, viciously stupid, senseless, except that the dry leaves were piling up higher and the gusts of wind were perhaps more frequent, and the sun was pouring more gold than ever onto that vile heap of garbage. It was simply unbearable. And then all of a sudden the public prosecutor started running—it was like a release, a liberation—broke through the undergrowth, straight toward the child, ignoring the fact that his shoes were sinking into the ashes, and as we saw him stomping up to the girl, we, too, burst out of our cover; it was time to put an end to this.

"'Who are you waiting for?' the public prosecutor screamed at the girl, who sat on her stone, clutching her doll and staring up at him in terror.

"'Who are you waiting for, damn it, answer me now!'

"And now we had all reached the girl and surrounded her, and she stared at us in utter horror and incomprehension.

"'Annemarie,' I said, and my voice was quivering with rage, 'a week ago someone gave you some chocolate. I'm sure you remember, little pieces of chocolate that looked like hedgehogs. Did a man in black clothes give them to you?'

"The girl did not answer. She just looked at me with tears in her eyes.

"Now Matthäi knelt down before her and put his arms around her little shoulders. 'Look, Annemarie,' he explained, 'you must tell us who gave you the chocolate. You must tell us exactly what that man looked like. I once knew a girl,' he continued urgently, for now everything was at stake, 'a girl who wore a red dress just like yours, and a big man in black clothes gave her chocolate. The same spiky little chocolate balls you ate. And then the girl went to the woods with that big man, and the big man killed the girl with a knife.'

"He fell silent. The girl still did not reply. She stared at him with wide-open eyes.

"'Annemarie,' Matthäi screamed, 'you must tell me the truth! All I want is to keep you from getting hurt!'

"'You're lying,' the girl quietly replied. 'You're lying.'

"Now the public prosecutor lost his patience for the second time. 'You stupid brat,' he yelled, grabbing the child's arm and shaking her, 'now tell us what you know!' And we all shouted with him, senselessly, because we had simply lost control of ourselves; we, too, shook her, and started to hit her, beat that little body lying there in ashes and red leaves among rusty tin cans, beat her cruelly, furiously, shouting and yelling.

"The girl let our fury pass over her for what seemed an eternity, though it must have lasted only a few seconds, and

126

made no sound at all. But then suddenly she screamed with such an unearthly, inhuman voice that we stood frozen to the spot. 'You're lying! You're lying! You're lying!' Appalled, we let her go. Her screams had brought us back to our senses, and we were filled with horror and shame at what we had done.

"'We're animals,' I gasped. 'We're beasts.'

"The child ran across the clearing to the edge of the forest. 'You're lying! You're lying! You're lying!' she shrieked again, so horribly we thought she had lost her mind, but she ran straight into the arms of her mother. For Lotte Heller—as if things hadn't gone from bad to worse already—had just at that moment stepped into the clearing. That was all we needed. She was informed about everything; the teacher had talked after all when Lotte walked past the school; I knew it, I didn't have to ask. And now this creature of doom stood there, hugging her sobbing child, and staring at us with the same look her daughter had given us before. Naturally she knew every one of us—Feller, Henzi, and unfortunately the public prosecutor, too; the situation was grotesquely awkward; we were all embarrassed and felt plainly ridiculous; the whole thing was nothing but a lousy miserable comedy. 'Lies! Lies! Lies!' the child was still screaming, beside herself. 'Lies! Lies! Lies!' Then Matthäi went up to the two of them, head bowed, with uncertain steps.

"'Fräulein Heller,' he said politely, humbly in fact, which made no sense at all, because there was only one thing left to do, and that was to put an end to the whole thing, finish, case closed, cut loose from the whole bloody puzzle, no matter whether the murderer existed or not. 'Fräulein Heller, I noticed

127

that Annemarie was given chocolate by an unknown person. I have reason to suspect that this is the same person who lured a little girl into a forest a few weeks ago and killed her.'

"He spoke precisely and in such an officious manner I could have laughed out loud. The woman calmly looked into his eyes. Then she spoke just as formally and politely as Matthäi. 'Inspector,' she asked softly, 'did you take me and Annemarie into your gas station just so you could find this person?'

"'There was no other way, Fräulein Heller,' the inspector replied.

"'You are a swine,' the woman quietly replied, without moving a muscle in her face. Then she took her child and went through the woods in the direction of the gas station."

27

"We stood there in the clearing, in the lengthening shadows, surrounded by old tin cans and tangled wire, our feet in ashes and leaves. It was all over, our whole undertaking had turned into a senseless, ridiculous mess, in fact nothing less than a catastrophe. Matthäi was the only one who had regained his composure. He looked downright stiff and dignified in his blue mechanic's outfit. He performed a tight little bow before the public prosecutor—I could hardly believe my eyes and ears—and said: 'Herr Burkhard, now we must keep on waiting. There is no other way. We must wait, wait, and wait again. If you would give me six more men and the radio equipment, that would be enough.'

"The public prosecutor eyed my former subordinate with alarm. He had come prepared for everything but this. Just a moment ago he had firmly intended to give us all an earful; now he gulped a few times, passed a hand over his forehead, and then abruptly turned on his heels and stomped with Henzi through the woods in the direction of the gas station. At a sign from me, Feller also left.

"Matthäi and I were alone.

"'Now you listen to me,' I shouted, determined to bring the man to his senses at last, and furious at myself for supporting his nonsense, indeed for making it possible.

"'The operation has failed, we have to admit that. We waited more than a week and no one showed up.'

"Matthäi did not answer. He just looked about, peering, listening. Then he went to the edge of forest, walked around the clearing, and returned. I was still standing on the garbage heap, up to my ankles in ashes.

"'The girl was waiting for him,' he said.

"I shook my head. 'No,' I said. 'The girl came here to be by herself, to sit by the brook, to dream with her doll, and to sing 'Maria sat upon a stone.' We just imagined that she was waiting for someone.'

"Matthäi listened attentively to my words.

"'Someone gave Annemarie the hedgehogs,' he said stubbornly, still firmly convinced.

"'Someone gave Annemarie some chocolate,' I said. 'That's true. Anyone could give chocolate to a child! But that those chocolate truffles were the hedgehogs in Gritli Moser's drawing—I'm sorry, Matthäi, that, too, is your interpretation, and there's nothing to prove it.'

"Again Matthäi gave no response. He walked back to the edge of the forest, circled the clearing again, searched a spot where fallen leaves had accumulated, then gave up and returned to me.

"'This is the site for a murder,' he said. 'You can feel it. I will keep waiting.'

"'But that's nonsense,' I replied, suddenly filled with horror and disgust. I was shivering, exhausted.

"'He will come here,' Matthäi said.

"I screamed at him, beside myself: 'This is complete nonsense! It's idiotic!'

"He seemed not to be listening. 'Let's go back to the gas station,' he said.

"I was more than glad to turn my back on that accursed place. The sun stood low now, the shadows were tremendous, the wide valley lay steeped in a strong golden glow, and the sky above was a pure blue; but I hated everything. I felt as though I had been exiled to some huge, awful postcard world. Then the highway appeared—rolling cars, convertibles with colorfully dressed people, the wealth of life surging and roaring past. It was absurd. We reached the gas station. Feller was waiting in my car next to the pumps. He was half-asleep again. Annemarie was sitting on her swing, singing in a tinny, somewhat tearful voice, 'Maria sat upon a stone,' and there was a fellow standing there, leaning against the doorpost, probably a worker from the brickyard, with an open shirt and a hairy chest, a cigarette in his mouth, grinning. Matthäi ignored him. He went into the little room, to the table where we had sat before; I trotted after him. He put a bottle of schnapps on the table and poured himself one glass after the other. I couldn't drink, I was too disgusted by everything. Lotte Heller was nowhere in sight.

"'It'll be hard,' he said, 'but the clearing isn't that far. Or do you think I'd better wait here, by the gas station?'

"I didn't answer him. Matthäi walked back and forth, drank, and ignored my silence.

"'It's too bad Annemarie and her mother found out,' he said. 'But we'll fix that.'

"Outside, the noise of the road and the child's whining voice: 'Maria sat upon a stone.'

"'I'm leaving now, Matthäi,' I said.

"He went on drinking, didn't even look at me.

"'Good-bye,' I said, left the room, stepped outside, walked past the man and the little girl, and waved to Feller, startling him out of his half sleep. He opened the door of the car for me.

"'Back to headquarters,' I ordered."

28

"That's the story as far as poor old Matthäi figures in it," the former chief of the cantonal police continued. (This is probably the right place to mention the fact that the old man and I had long since finished our drive from Chur to Zurich and were now sitting in the Kronenhalle, the restaurant he had mentioned and praised so often in his account, being served by Emma, of course, under the painting by Gubler—which had replaced the Miró—all in accord with the old man's habits and preference. I should mention, too, that we had already eaten—off the trolley, *bollito milanese;* this, too, was one of his traditions, why not go along with it; it was nearly four o'clock already, and after the "Café Partagas," as the chief called his passion for smoking a Havana along with his espresso and following these up with a Réserve du Patron, he offered me a second charlotte. I should also add, as a purely technical point, in defense of my craft and for the sake of literary honesty, that I have of course not always reproduced that immense verbal outpouring precisely as it was delivered, and I'm not just referring to the fact that we spoke in Swiss dialect; I mean those parts of the old man's story which he did not relate from his own point of view, as his own experience, but described objectively, as events in themselves—for example the scene when Matthäi gave his

133

solemn promise. At such moments I had to intervene, shape and reshape, though I took the greatest pains not to falsify anything but only to take the material the old man supplied and rework it according to certain laws of the writer's craft; in short, to put it into publishable form.)

"Naturally," he continued, "I went back to visit Matthäi a few times, more and more convinced he had been mistaken about the peddler's innocence, because in the following months, and eventually years, no new murder took place. Well, I don't have to go into further detail; the man fell apart, drank himself into a perpetual stupor, degenerated; there was no way to help him or bring about a change; at night, the young fellows no longer slinked and whistled around the gas station in vain; things took a nasty turn, the Graubünden police made a number of raids. I had to fill them in on the whole story; once my colleagues in Chur understood, they looked the other way. They've always been more sensible up there than we are. So everything took its fatal course, and you saw the results yourself a few hours ago. It's a sad story. Especially because the little girl, Annemarie, didn't turn out any better than her mother. Possibly just because various organizations immediately leaped to her aid—foster homes and the like. She was taken care of, but kept running away and coming back to the gas station, where Lotte Heller set up that shabby bar two years ago. God only knows how she wangled the license; at any rate, that finished the kid. She pitched in. In every respect. Four months ago she came back after a year of reform school. Not that she learned anything from it. You saw her with your own eyes, let's not dwell on it. But I bet you've been wondering all this time what my story has to do with the criticism I made of your lecture, and why I called Matthäi a genius. A very reasonable question. Your objection is probably that a wild and ingenious hunch isn't necessarily right, let alone inspired. That, too, is correct. I can even imagine what you're cooking up in your literary brain. All we need—I can imagine you making some sly calculation like this—all we need is for Matthäi to be on the right track, let him capture the murderer in the end, and bingo, we've got a terrific novel or movie script. After all, what's the purpose of writing if not to give things a certain twist that'll make them transparent, so that the higher idea shines through just enough for the reader to sense it, infer it; in fact, by this little twist, by making Matthäi succeed, my degenerate detective would become not just interesting, he'd be a character of biblical dimensions, a sort of modern Abraham of hope and faith, and my senseless story—of someone who goes after a nonexistent murderer because he believes in the innocence of a guilty man—would be full of meaning; thus the guilty peddler would become innocent in the realm of poetic vision, the nonexistent murderer would become a real one, and a course of events that tends to make a mockery of human faith and human reason would instead glorify these powers. Who cares what actually happened, and how; the main thing is that this version is equally possible. That, more or less, is how I imagine your train of thought, and I can predict that this variant of my story is so uplifting and positive that it will just have to be published or turned into a film in the near future. You will tell it all pretty much the way I tried to, but you'll make it more understandable. After, all, you're a pro. You won't let the murderer show up until the very end; that way, hope is rewarded, faith triumphs, and the story becomes acceptable for the Christian world. I could imagine a few other softening touches. For example, I would suggest that as soon as Matthäi discovers the truffles, he is shocked into awareness of Anne-marie's dangerous situation and is no longer able to continue with his plan of using the child as bait—either out of mature altruism or out of paternal love, whereupon he could take Annemarie and her mother out of harm's way and put a big doll next to the little brook. Then a huge, solemn figure would come striding out of the forest, straight up to the look-alike doll—Annemarie's wizard, lusting for this new chance to apply his razor; then, realizing he had fallen into a diabolic trap, he would fly into a rage, a fit of madness, there'd be a fight with Matthäi and the police, and then perhaps at the end—please bear with me, I'm just trying to imagine—there'd be a deeply moving conversation between the wounded inspector and the child, not long, just a few fragmentary sentences. Why not? You could have the girl slip away from her mother to meet her beloved wizard, race through the woods toward her great happiness; that way, after all those horrors, you could pierce the darkness with a ray of gentle humanity, sweet renunciation, and poetic tenderness; or else, more likely, you'll fabricate something very different; I know you a little by now, even though, to be perfectly frank, I prefer Max Frisch; it'll be the very senselessness of my story that appeals to you, the fact that someone believes in the innocence of a guilty man and now sets out to find a murderer who cannot exist, as we have defined the situation accurately enough. But now you become cruder than reality; just for the hell of it and to make us policemen look completely ridiculous: now Matthäi would actually find a murderer, one of your comical saints, some sectarian preacher with a heart of gold who is, of course, innocent and utterly incapable of doing anything evil, and just for that reason, by one of your more malicious inventions, he would attract every shred of suspicion the plot has to offer. Matthäi would kill this pure, simple soul, all his proofs would be confirmed, whereupon we at headquarters would take the happy detective back into our fold and celebrate him as a genius. That's another conceivable version. You see, I'm onto you. But I expect you won't just ascribe all my talk to the Réserve du Patron—though we're into our second bottle, admittedly; no, I presume you have a feeling that I have yet to tell the end of the story; with some reluctance, I must say, because unfortunately—I don't have to hide this from you—unfortunately this story has a point, and as you no doubt already suspect, that point is a thoroughly shabby one, so shabby that it simply can't be used in any decent novel or film. It is so ridiculous, stupid, and trivial, it would ruin the story, you would just have to skip it. However, it would be dishonest not to admit that this point is, for now at least, thoroughly in Mattäi's favor, puts him in the proper light, and makes him a genius, a person so deeply attuned to aspects of reality that are hidden from us that he broke through the hypotheses and assumptions that obstruct our vision and penetrated close to those laws that keep the world in motion, and which always elude our grasp. He came close, but no nearer than that. For this gruesome point which, I'm very sorry to say, is a real part of my story—this factor of the incalculable, this randomness, if you will—makes all his genius, his plans, and his actions appear even more painfully absurd in hindsight than was the case before, when in the opinion of all of us at headquarters he was mistaken: there is no greater cruelty than a genius stumbling over something idiotic. But when something like that happens, everything depends on the stance the genius takes toward the ridiculous thing that tripped him; whether he can accept it or not. Matthäi couldn't accept it. He wanted reality to conform to his calculations. Therefore he had to deny reality and end in a void. So my story ends on a particularly sad note—it's just about the most banal of all the possible 'solutions.' Sometimes that just happens. Sometimes the worst possible thing *does* take place. We are men, we have to reckon with that, armor ourselves against it, and above all, we have to realize that the only way to avoid getting crushed by absurdity, which is bound to manifest itself more and more forcefully and clearly, and the only way to make a reasonably comfortable home for ourselves on this earth, is to humbly include the absurd in our calculations. Our rational mind casts only a feeble light on the world. In the twilight of its borders live the ghosts of paradox. Let us beware of taking these figments as things existing 'in themselves,' independently of the human mind; or, even worse: let us not make the mistake of regarding them as an error that can be avoided, which could tempt us to execute the world out of some sort of defiant morality once we made the attempt to establish a flawless rational structure, for its very perfection would be its deadly lie and a sign of the most terrible blindness. But forgive me for injecting this commentary into my lovely story. Philosophically not quite up to par, I know, but you have to grant an old man like me a few thoughts about what he's experienced, crude though they may be; I'm just a policeman, but still I do make an effort to be a man and not an ox."

29

"Well, it was last year—on a Sunday again, naturally—that I received a telephone call from a Catholic priest and had to pay a visit to the cantonal hospital. It happened just before my retirement, in the last days of my term in office. My successor was already on the job—not Henzi, who fortunately didn't make it, despite his well-connected wife—but a man of substance and rigor, endowed with a civil decency that could only be of benefit to the office he held. The telephone call had reached me in my apartment. The only reason I acceded to the request was that it was supposed to be something important a dying woman wanted to tell me, which is something that happens now and then. It was a sunny but cold December day. Everything bare, forlorn, melancholy. At such moments our city can reduce you to tears. What a day! As if visiting a dying woman wasn't depressing enough. That's why I walked around Aeschbacher's *Harp* in the park several times, in a rather gloomy mood, but finally I pulled myself together and walked into the building. Frau Schrott, medical clinic, private ward. The room, with a view to the park, was full of flowers, roses, gladioli. The curtains were half-drawn. Slanting rays of light fell on the floor. By the window sat a huge priest with a rough red face and a gray untended beard, and in the bed lay a little old woman, delicately wrinkled, her hair thin and snow white, extraordinarily gentle, apparently very rich, to judge by the care she was receiving. Next to the bed stood a complicated apparatus, some sort of medical contraption with various hoses that led under her blanket. The machine had to be repeatedly checked by a nurse who kept walking in and out of the room, silent and observant. I might as well mention these regular interruptions right at the start.

"I said hello. The old woman looked at me attentively and very calmly. Her face was waxen, unreal, but still curiously animated. In her wrinkled yellowish hands she was holding a little black gilt-edged book, evidently a psalter, but it was almost impossible to believe that this woman was about to die; such a vital, unbroken force emanated from her, despite all those tubes crawling out from under her blanket. The priest remained seated. With a gesture as majestic as it was awkward he indicated a chair next to the bed.

"'Sit down,' he said, and when I had taken the seat, his deep voice sounded again from the window, before which he towered as a mighty silhouette. 'Tell the chief what you have to report, Frau Schrott. At eleven we'll have to proceed with Extreme Unction.'

"Frau Schrott smiled. 'I'm sorry to put you to so much trouble,' she said with great charm, and her voice, although quiet, was still very clear, in fact quite lively.

"'It's no trouble at all,' I lied, convinced now that the old woman was going to inform me of some bequest for needy policemen or something like that.

"'It's a rather unimportant and harmless story I have to tell you,' the old woman continued, 'the sort of thing that probably happens in all families once or several times, which is why I forgot it, but now that eternity is drawing near, I suppose it had to come up again. I mentioned it in my general confession, purely by chance, because a moment before, a granddaughter of my only godchild had come with flowers and wearing a little red skirt, and Father Beck got all upset and told me to tell you the story, I really don't know why, it's all in the past, but if Reverend Beck thinks—'

"'Tell him what happened, Frau Schrott,' said the deep voice by the window, 'tell him.' And in the city the church bells started ringing the end of the sermon, a dark, distant clanging.

"'Well, I'll try,' the old woman began again, and started to chatter. 'It's been such a long time since I've told a story. I used to tell stories to Emil, my first husband's son, but then Emil died of consumption, there was nothing anyone could do. He would have been as old as I am now. Or rather, as old as Reverend Beck. But now I'll try to imagine that you're my son, and that Reverend Beck is my son, too. Because right after Emil, I gave birth to Markus, but he died three days after he was born, premature. He was a six-month baby, and Dr. Hobler thought it was best for the poor little thing.' And on and on she went in this scattered manner.

"'Tell the story, Frau Schrott, tell it,' the priest admonished her in his bass voice, sitting immobile by the window except for an occasional Moses-like movement of his hand as he stroked his wild gray beard, emitting all the while a distinct succession of mild, steady waves imbued with the odor of garlic. 'We don't have much time. We have to proceed with Extreme Unction!'

"Now she suddenly became proud, downright aristocratic. She even raised her little head a bit, and her eyes flashed. 'I am a Stänzli,' she said. 'My grandfather was Colonel Stänzli, who led the retreat to Escholzmatt in the Sonderbund War, and my sister married Colonel Stüssi of the Zurich General Staff in the First World War, who was General Ulrich Wille's best friend and knew Kaiser Wilhelm personally, as I'm sure you remember.'

"'Of course,' I said, feeling bored, 'naturally.' What did I care about old Wille and Kaiser Wilhelm? Spit it out already, I said silently in my thoughts, to whom do you want to bequeath your money? If only I could smoke, a Suerdieck cigarillo would be just the right thing to blow some jungle air into this hospital atmosphere and these damn garlic waves. And the priest droned on like the bass register of a giant organ, stubbornly, relentlessly: 'Tell the story, Frau Schrott, tell the story.'

"'You should know,' the old lady continued, and now her face took on a strangely fierce, almost hateful expression, 'you should know that my sister with her Colonel Stüssli were to blame for the whole thing. My sister is ten years older than I, she's ninety-nine now, she's been a widow for forty years, she's got a villa on the Zurichberg, she's got Brown-Boveri stock, she owns half the Bahnhofstrasse. . . .' And then suddenly, out of the mouth of this little old lady on her deathbed, came a muddy stream, or let's put it this way: such a filthy, squalid flood of profanity that I wouldn't dare to reproduce it. At the same time the old creature raised herself slightly, and her little ancient head with the snow-white hair wiggled back and forth with astonishing vigor, as if mad with joy over

143

this burst of rage. But then she calmed down again, because fortunately the nurse came in—now, now, Frau Schrott, let's not get upset, nice and easy now. The old woman obeyed, and made a feeble movement with her hand when we were alone again.

"'All these flowers,' she said, 'they're from my sister. She sends them just to annoy me. She knows very well I don't like flowers. I hate to see money wasted like that. But we never had a falling-out, as you probably imagine. No, no, we have always been sweet and kind to each other. All the Stänzlis have this politeness, even though we can't stand one another. You see, we use our politeness to hurt each other. Oh, if we could draw blood with politeness, we would. And a good thing it is, this discipline in the family, because otherwise all hell would break loose.'

"'The story, Frau Schrott,' the priest urged again for a change. 'Extreme Unction is waiting.' By now, in my wish for something to smoke, I had replaced the little Suerdieck with one of my big Bahianos.

"The endless babbling flood continued: 'Back in '95, I married Dr. Galuser, God bless his dear departed soul, he was a physician in Chur. That fact alone was an affront to my sister with her colonel, my husband wasn't a fine enough gentleman for them, I could definitely tell, and when the colonel died of influenza later, right after the First World War, my sister got more and more unbearable. She practically sainted her fancy militarist, it was disgusting.'

"'Tell the story, Frau Schrott, the story,' the priest kept after her, but not at all impatiently; at most, he betrayed a faint

144

sadness at so much confusion. I was drifting. Once in a while his voice startled me out of my stupor: 'Extreme Unction's coming soon, get to the point, tell the story.'

"There was nothing to be done; the old woman went on nattering away on her deathbed, sliding from one subject into the next, inexhaustibly, despite her feeble, high-pitched voice and the tubes beneath her blanket. To the extent that I was still able to think, I vaguely expected some banal story about a helpful policeman, and then the announcement of a bequest of a few thousand francs, just to annoy the ninety-nine-year-old sister; I prepared some warm words of gratitude, and in order not to succumb to despair altogether, I resolutely suppressed my unrealistic dreams of a good smoke and yearned for my customary aperitif and the traditional Sunday dinner in the Kronenhalle with my wife and daughter.

"'And then,' the old woman continued, 'after the death of my dear departed husband, the late Dr. Galuser, I married the late Herr Schrott, who used to be our chauffeur and gardener and general handyman; yes, he did all the things that have to be done in a big old house and that really ought to be done by men, like heating, fixing the shutters, and so forth, and even though my sister made no comment about it and even came to Chur for the wedding, I know she was angry about this marriage. Not that my sister would ever show it, oh no, she wouldn't give me that pleasure. Anyway, that's how I became Frau Schrott.'

"She sighed. Outside, somewhere in the corridor, the nurses were singing. Christmas carols. 'Well, it was quite a harmonious marriage with my dearly beloved,' the dying woman continued after listening to a few bars of the song. 'Even though it was probably harder for him than I can imagine. My blessed Albert was twenty-three when we married—since he had been born in 1900 exactly—and I was already fifty-five. But I'm sure it was the best thing he could do. You see, he was an orphan; his mother was—oh, I don't want to even say what she was, and as for his father, nobody knew who he was, not even his name. My first husband had taken the boy in when he was sixteen; he couldn't cope with school, you know, he never was much good at reading and writing. Marriage was simply the cleanest solution. As a widow, you see, you get talked about; not that there was ever anything between me and Albie, bless his dear soul, not when we were married either, how could there have been, with such a great difference in age; but my assets were limited, I had to keep a budget in order to get by with the rent I collected from my houses in Zurich and Chur; but imagine my blessed Albie, with his limited mental capacities, having to go out and fend for himself in the struggle of life—he would have been lost, and as a Christian one does have certain obligations. So we lived together honorably; he did this and that in the house and the garden, a good-looking man, I have to say, a big, firm fellow, always dressed in a dignified way, as if for a formal occasion; I never had cause to be ashamed of him, even though he hardly said anything, except maybe, "Yes, Mumsy, of course, Mumsy," but he was obedient and temperate in his drinking; not with food though, he loved to eat, especially noodles, all sorts of pasta in fact, and chocolate. That was his passion, chocolate. But for the rest, he was a good, decent man and stayed that way all his life, so much nicer and so much more obedient than the chauffeur my sister married four years later, despite her colonel. He, too, was only thirty.'

"The old woman fell silent, apparently exhausted, while I innocently awaited the bequest for needy policemen.

"'Tell the story, Frau Schrott,' the priest's voice wafted from the window with relentless indifference.

"Frau Schrott nodded. 'You see, Chief,' she said, 'in the forties my life with Bertie gradually started to go downhill, I'm not sure what was wrong with him, but something must have been damaged in his head; he got more and more blank and quiet, stared into space a lot, didn't speak for days at a time, only did his work, always properly so I had no reason to scold him, but he would drive around for hours on his bicycle. Maybe the war confused him, or the fact that the army hadn't taken him; who's to say what goes on in a man's head! Also, he was eating a tremendous amount; fortunately we had our chickens and rabbits. And then that thing happened to my dear departed Albert, the thing I'm supposed to tell you about. The first time was near the end of the war.'

"She stopped talking because once again the nurse and a doctor had entered the room. They busied themselves in part behind the medical contraption, in part behind the old woman. The doctor was German, blond, straight out of a picture book, cheerful, peppy, on his routine round as the doctor on Sunday service, how are you, Frau Schrott, chin up, my, my, you've got excellent results, don't give up now; then he strode away, followed by the nurse, and the priest admonished the patient: 'Tell the story, Frau Schrott, Extreme

147

Unction's at eleven,' a prospect that did not seem to alarm the old biddy in the least.

"She resumed her tale: 'Every week my poor little Albie, God bless his soul, had to bring eggs to my militarist sister in Zurich. He would tie the little basket to the back of his bicycle and come back in the evening, because he would start out early, at five or six in the morning, always dressed up in black, with a round hat. Everyone gave him a friendly greeting when he pedaled through Chur and then out into the country, whistling his favorite song, "I am a Switzer lad and love my country dear."

This time it was a hot midsummer day, two days after the national holiday, and this time it was past midnight when he came home. I heard him fussing and washing in the bathroom for a long time, went there, and saw my dear Bertie all covered with blood, his clothes, too. "My God, Bertie," I asked, "what happened to you?" He just stared, and then he said, "An accident, Mumsy, I'll be all right, go to sleep, Mumsy," so I went to sleep, even though I wondered because I hadn't seen any wounds. But in the morning, when we were having breakfast and he was eating his eggs, always four at a time, and his slices of bread with marmalade, I read in the newspaper that a little girl had been murdered in the canton of St. Gallen, probably with a razor, and then it occurred to me that in the bathroom the night before, he had been cleaning his razor, even though he always shaved in the morning, and then I suddenly realized what had happened, it came like a revelation, and I got very serious with Albie, God bless his soul, and said, "Albie dear, you killed that girl in St. Gallen

148

canton, didn't you?" Then he stopped eating his eggs and bread and marmalade and pickles and said, "Yes, Mumsy, it had to be, it was a voice from heaven," and then he went on eating. I was all confused that he could be so sick; I felt sorry for the girl, I also thought of calling Dr. Sichler, not the old one but his son, who is also very capable and very sympathetic; but then I thought of my sister, she would have been tickled pink, it would have been the best day of her life, so I was just very stern and firm with my blessed Albie and told him plainly: "This must never, never happen again," and he said, "Yes, Mumsy." "How did it happen?" I asked. "Mumsy," he said, "I kept meeting a little girl with a red skirt and blond braids when I drove to Zurich by way of Wattwil, a big detour, but ever since I met this girl near a little patch of woods I always had to take the detour, the voice from heaven, Mumsy, and the voice told me to share my chocolate with her, and then I had to kill the girl, it was all the voice from heaven, Mumsy, and then I went into the woods nearby and lay under a shrub until night came, and then I came back to you, Mumsy." "Albie," I said, "you're not going to drive your bicycle to my sister anymore; we'll send the eggs by mail." "Yes, Mumsy," he said, smeared some jam on another slice of bread, and went into the courtyard. I suppose now I really should go to Father Beck, I thought, so he'd give my blessed Albie a serious talking-to, but then I looked out the window, and seeing my blessed Albie so faithfully doing his duty out there in the sun, quietly and a little sadly mending the rabbit hutch, and seeing how spick-and-span the whole courtyard was, I thought, "What's done is done, Albie is a good, decent fellow, and basically such a kind soul, and besides, it won't happen again."'

"Now the nurse came back into the room, checked the instrument, rearranged the tubes, and the little old woman lying back in her pillow seemed exhausted again. I hardly dared to breathe. The sweat was running down my face; I ignored it. I was suddenly cold and felt doubly ridiculous for having expected a bequest from the old woman. And then this enormous array of flowers, all those red and white roses, flaming gladioli, asters, zinnias, carnations, obtained God knows where, a whole vaseful of orchids, senseless, blatant, and the sun behind the curtains, and that huge motionless priest, and the smell of garlic; I felt like flying into a rage, arresting the woman, but it would have been pointless, she was about to receive Extreme Unction, and there I sat in my Sunday suit, all spiffed up and useless.

"'Go on with the story, Frau Schrott,' the priest admonished impatiently, 'get on with it.' And she went on. 'And so my dear blessed Albert really did get better,' she expounded in her calm, gentle voice, and it really was as if she were telling two children a fairy tale in which evil and absurdity happen just like goodness and just as wonderful. 'He no longer went to Zurich; but when the Second World War was over, we could use our car again, the one I had bought back in '38, because the car of Dr. Galuser, God bless his soul, was really out of fashion, and so Bertie, God bless his soul, drove me around in our Buick again. Once we even went to Ascona, and then I thought, Since he gets so much pleasure from driving, why not let him go to Zurich again, it's not so dangerous with the

Buick, he'll have to keep his eye on the road and won't hear any voices from heaven, and so he was driving out to my sister again and faithfully delivering the eggs like a good boy, and every once in a while he delivered a rabbit. But then unfortunately one day he didn't come home until after midnight. I immediately went to the garage; I sensed it right away, because he had suddenly started taking chocolate truffles from the candy box, and sure enough I found Bertie, God bless his soul, washing the inside of his car, and everywhere I looked there was blood. "Did you kill a girl again, Bertie?" I said, in a very serious tone. "Mumsy," he said, "don't worry, it wasn't in the St. Gallen canton, it was in Schwyz canton, the voice from heaven wanted it, the girl had a red dress and blond braids again." But I *was* worried, and I was even sterner with him than the first time; I almost got angry. He wasn't allowed to drive the Buick for a week, and I wanted to go to Father Beck, I really intended to; but my sister would have been just delighted to hear that, I couldn't let that happen, and so I kept even stricter watch over Albert, God bless his soul, and then for two years things went really well, until he did it again, because he just had to obey the voice from heaven, my Albie, God bless his soul, he was crushed, he cried, but I noticed it right away because there were truffles missing from the bonbon box. This time it was a girl in the Zurich canton, again with a little red skirt and yellow braids. It's unbelievable, how carelessly mothers dress their children.'

"'Was the girl's name Gritli Moser?" I asked.

"'Her name was Gritli, and the ones before were Sonya and Eveli,' the old lady replied. 'I noted all the names; but

151

Albie, God bless his soul, got worse and worse, he started to get absentminded, I had to tell him everything ten times, all day long I had to scold him like a schoolboy, and it was in 1949 or fifty, I'm not sure any longer, a few months after Gritli, that he started getting restless again, and jumpy; even the chicken coop was a mess, and the chickens were cackling wildly because he wasn't feeding them properly, and he kept driving around in our Buick and staying away for whole afternoons, just saying he was out for a ride, and suddenly I noticed there were truffles missing in the bonbon box. Then I watched him closely, and when he stole into the living room, my Albie, God bless his soul, with his razor tucked into a pocket like a fountain pen, I went up to him and said: "Albie, you found another girl." "The voice from heaven, Mumsy," he replied, "please let me do it just this one time; it's commanded by heaven, I have to obey, and she has a red skirt, too, and blond braids." "Albie," I said sternly, "I can't allow this, where is the girl?" "Not far from here, near a gas station," Albie said, God bless his soul. "Please, please, Mumsy, let me obey." Then I put my foot down: "Absolutely not, Albie," I said, "you gave me your promise; now clean the chicken coop and give the chickens a decent feeding." Then Albie, God bless his soul, got angry, for the first time in our marriage, which was so harmonious otherwise, he shouted: "All I am is your servant," that's how sick he was, and ran out with the truffles and the razor to the Buick, and just fifteen minutes later I received a call telling me he had collided with a truck and died. His Reverence Beck came and Police Captain Bühler, he was particularly sensitive, which is why in my testament I have bequeathed five thousand francs to the police in Chur, and five thousand more will be going to the Zurich police, because I have houses here in the Freistrasse, and of course my sister came with her chauffeur, just to annoy me. She spoiled the whole funeral for me.'

"I stared at the old woman. There it was, the bequest I had been waiting for. It felt like a mockery.

"But now finally the head doctor came with an assistant and two nurses; we were sent out, and I took leave of Frau Schrott.

"'Good-bye, stay well,' I said stupidly, feeling embarrassed and wanting nothing more than to get away as quickly as possible, whereupon she started to giggle and the head doctor gave me a peculiar look; the scene was awkward, to say the least; I was glad to leave the old woman, the priest, the whole assembly behind me and finally step out into the hallway.

"Everywhere I looked, there were visitors with packages and flowers. Everything smelled of hospital. I fled. The exit was near; in my mind, I was already outside in the park. But then a very large man in dark, formal clothes with a round, childish face and a hat came down the corridor pushing a wheelchair in which sat a wrinkled, trembling old woman in a mink coat, holding flowers in both arms, enormous bundles of them. Maybe this was the ninety-nine-year-old sister with her chauffeur, what did I know? I looked after them in horror until they vanished in the private ward. Then I almost ran. I rushed out of the building and through the park, past patients in wheelchairs, past convalescents, past visitors, and only began to calm down in the Kronenhalle. Over the liver dumpling soup."

30

"I drove straight from the Kronenhalle to Chur. Unfortunately I had to take my wife and daughter along; it was Sunday and I had promised them the afternoon, and I didn't want to get embroiled in explanations. I didn't say a word, drove way above the speed limit; maybe something could still be salvaged. But my family didn't have to wait long in the car outside the gas station. The tavern was positively hopping. Annemarie had just come back from reform school; the place was swarming with some pretty unsavory characters; despite the cold, Matthäi was sitting on his bench in his mechanic's overalls, smoking a cheroot, stinking of absinthe. I sat down beside him and told him the story in a few words. But it was too late. He didn't even seem to be listening. For a moment I was decided; then I went back to my Opel Kapitän and drove on to Chur. My family was impatient, they were hungry.

"'Wasn't that Matthäi?' my wife asked; as usual, she had no idea.

"'Yes.'

"'I thought he was in Jordan,' she said.

"'He didn't go, dear.'

"In Chur we had trouble parking. The pastry shop was crammed full of people from Zurich and their screaming children, all stuffing their bellies and sweating. But finally we found a table, ordered tea and pastry. But my wife called the waitress back again.

"'And please bring us half a pound of chocolate truffles.'

"She was only slightly surprised when I didn't want to eat any truffles. Not for the life of me.

"And now, my dear sir, you can do what you want with this story. Emma, the bill."

———

▼ Did you know?

Swiss writer Friedrich Dürrenmatt was one of the most highly regarded German-language novelists and dramatists of the twentieth century, and his works have been translated into 49 languages. As a dramatist he wrote plays that reflected the mood of a war-scarred Europe. As a novelist, he is famed for his philosophical crime thrillers, which draw comparisons to the works of Paul Auster and Umberto Eco for their post-modern questioning of the conventions of the genre.

Dürrenmatt thought detective novels should reflect the absurdity of real life rather than proceeding like mathematical equations with a definite solution. Of the traditional crime writers, he once said, "You set up your stories logically, like a chess game: all the detective needs to know is the rules, he replays the moves of the game, and checkmate, the criminal is caught and justice has triumphed. This fantasy drives me crazy."

Dürrenmatt's most famous novel, *The Pledge*, was initially written as a screenplay titled *Es geschah am hellichten Tag* (*It Happened in Broad Daylight*). The film producers compelled Dürrenmatt to bring this original to a neat conclusion that they felt was more suitable for the screen. The decidedly un-neat conclusion of the subsequent novel, and the subtitle *Requiem for the Detective Novel*, reflect Dürrenmatt's deep dislike of such formulaic and predictable plot constructions. Ironically, this book went on to spawn two successful movies, including a 2001 film starring Jack Nicholson and directed by Sean Penn.

PUSHKIN VERTIGO

FRIEDRICH
DÜRRENMATT

AN INSPECTOR BARLACH MYSTERY

THE JUDGE AND
HIS HANGMAN

'SPELLBINDING' *WASHINGTON POST*

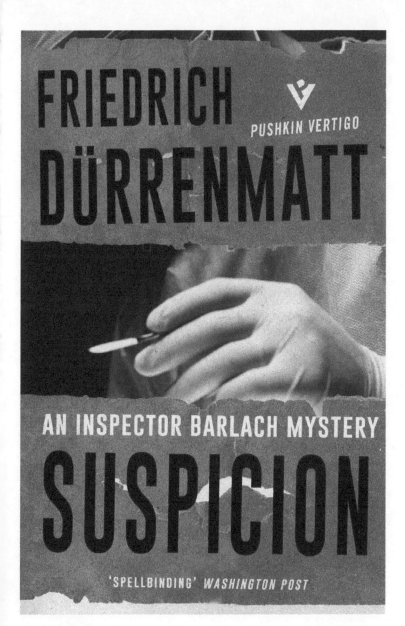

FRIEDRICH DÜRRENMATT

PUSHKIN VERTIGO

AN INSPECTOR BARLACH MYSTERY

SUSPICION

'SPELLBINDING' *WASHINGTON POST*

Find out more at **www.pushkinpress.com**